HOLD BACK
THE HUNTER

A NOVEL BY *Dale White*

The John Day Company • New York

© 1959 by Dale White

Library of Congress Catalogue
Card Number: 59-6722

To
Dr. Caroline McGill

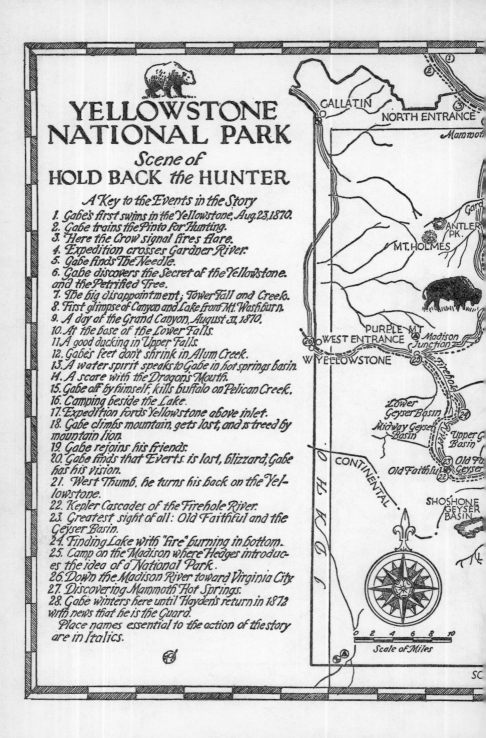

YELLOWSTONE NATIONAL PARK

Scene of
HOLD BACK the HUNTER

A Key to the Events in the Story

1. Gabe's first swims in the Yellowstone, Aug. 23, 1870.
2. Gabe trains the Pinto for Hunting.
3. Here the Crow signal fires flare.
4. Expedition crosses Gardner River.
5. Gabe finds The Needle.
6. Gabe discovers the Secret of the Yellowstone and the Petrified Tree.
7. The big disappointment; Tower Fall and Creek.
8. First glimpse of Canyon and Lake from Mt. Washburn.
9. A day at the Grand Canyon, August 31, 1870.
10. At the base of the Lower Falls.
11. A good ducking in Upper Falls.
12. Gabe's feet don't shrink in Alum Creek.
13. A water spirit speaks to Gabe in hot springs basin.
14. A scare with the Dragon's Mouth.
15. Gabe off by himself, kills buffalo on Pelican Creek.
16. Camping beside the Lake.
17. Expedition fords Yellowstone above inlet.
18. Gabe climbs mountain, gets lost, and is treed by mountain lion.
19. Gabe rejoins his friends.
20. Gabe finds that Everts is lost, blizzard; Gabe has his vision.
21. West Thumb, he turns his back on the Yellowstone.
22. Kepler Cascades of the Firehole River.
23. Greatest sight of all: Old Faithful and the Geyser Basin.
24. Finding Lake with "fire" burning in bottom.
25. Camp on the Madison where Hedges introduces the idea of a National Park.
26. Down the Madison River toward Virginia City.
27. Discovering Mammoth Hot Springs.
28. Gabe winters here until Hayden's return in 1872 with news that he is the Guard.

Place names essential to the action of the story are in Italics.

GALLATIN

NORTH ENTRANCE

Mammot

Gard

ANTLER PK.

MT. HOLMES

PURPLE MT

WEST ENTRANCE — Madison Junction

W. YELLOWSTONE

Lower Geyser Basin

Midway Geyser Basin

Upper G Basin

Old Faithful Geyser

Old Fa

CONTINENTAL

SHOSHONE GEYSER BASIN

Firehole River

I D A H O

0 2 4 6 8 10
Scale of Miles

SC

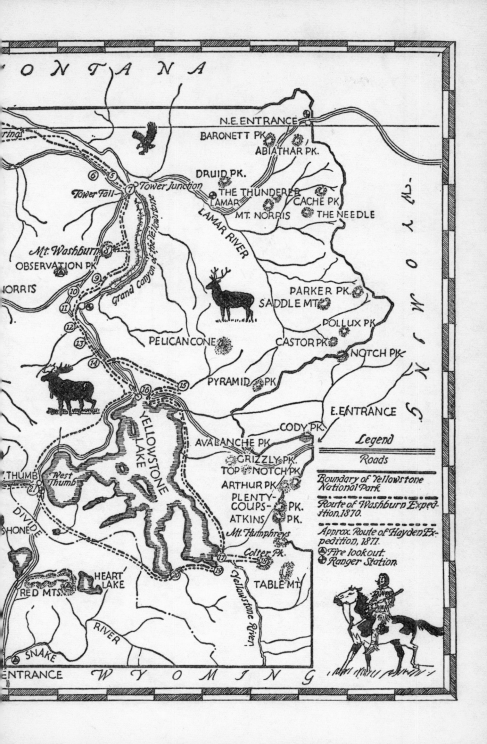

Contents

HOLD BACK THE HUNTER

I

You'll Never Come Out
of There Alive!

YOUNG Gabe Kirkpatrick plodded past the stores
fronting the lower side of Last Chance Gulch. The rough
planks slowed his walk to a mere shuffle. Occasionally
he stumbled going up the steps that were built into the
boardwalk every twenty paces or so. The straps of his
back pack cut into his shoulders, though the pack was
light enough by now. His buckskin leggings and shirt
clung to his thighs and back, sticky with sweat. There was
a damp ring under his cartridge belt and knife sheath.
Three months of travel (the last few days a forced march
over a hundred and forty miles of rough mountain country), had taken its toll, even of his young toughness.

Gabe was looking for Mr. Langford. The man back at
the saddler's had said, "Langford? The internal revenoo
collector?" With a calloused thumb he had pointed up the
gulch. "You want the buildin' with the green door, bud."

13

So Gabe had pushed on, every step a conscious effort. Langford. Langford. He had to find him before the expedition left for the Yellowstone. It was terribly important. Langford couldn't have gone yet—not after a fellow had come two thousand miles to see him.

There was no green door in the first block. It certainly was a noisy thoroughfare, this main street of Helena, thriving, bustling metropolis of the Montana Territory, August, 1870. The dust from the traffic and mining operations made him sneeze. Knee-booted miners tramped heavily alongside him and shouted greetings over his head. Ox teams bawled in their yokes as they hauled the heavy canvas-sheeted, squeaky-wheeled wagons along the rutted street. On the upper side of the gulch, where the mining claim markers stuck out like beads on the sinewy thread of the creek, a long line of men bent double over the gold pans or shoveled gravel into sluice boxes.

He peered at each two-story false front of the stores jammed wall to wall up the gulch. There was no green door in the second block either. The sun beat down on his bronzed face, beading it with perspiration. Without losing step or lowering the rifle cradled in his right arm, he slipped the sweatband off his forehead, mopped his face and neck, and put it on again, tucking his straight black hair behind his ears. He didn't want Mr. Langford to see him looking as greasy as a fresh-skinned bear.

Finally he spotted the green door. His heart beat a little faster as he opened it. At the end of a long dim hall he could see another door opening into an office. Inside at a desk sat a man, his back to a window flooded with sunshine. That must be Mr. Langford. At least he had brown

14

hair and a brown beard, the way Jim Bridger had described him.

Gabe stepped across the threshold and moved silently down the hallway. A few paces from the door he stopped to rub the toes of his moccasins so that the beadwork shone brightly. He wiped the walnut gunstock on his sleeve so Mr. Langford could see he was the kind of man who took care of a good gun. Then he ran his finger for the thousandth time along a secret pocket at the back of his rawhide knife sheath. Yes, the letter was still there. Everything that he wanted depended on the letter's reaching Mr. Langford.

He was about to move when he heard a man coming up behind him, his leather heels rapping noisily on the bare floor. As Gabe turned he could see the checkered suit and the hard round hat set back on his head, even in the dim light. The man shouldered Gabe aside and barged into the office. "Mr. Langford," Gabe couldn't help but hear, "I'm Tom Gerald of the *Helena Daily Herald*. The editor sent me to get a statement on your Yellowstone expedition. He's heard that practically all the members dropped out last night. Is it true the commandant at Fort Ellis telegraphed you that the Crows are on the rampage and threaten to massacre any party trespassing in the upper valley? Are you calling it quits?"

Gabe's back stiffened. He flattened himself against the wall so he could hear without being seen. It couldn't be! He hadn't traveled this far only to hear bad news. He held his breath, waiting for the answer.

"Not all of the men are dropping out!" Langford spoke vigorously.

15

The reporter seemed surprised. "How many? I mean, how many are going to make the trip?"

There would be nine of Helena's most prominent citizens, Mr. Langford answered a little stiffly, "not counting two wranglers and a cook."

"And me!" Gabe wanted to add, but didn't.

"I understand General Washburn has dropped out," the reporter added.

Mr. Langford said disgustedly, "I don't know where you pick up such rumors, Gerald, but they're absolutely false! General Washburn most certainly has not withdrawn. Nor has Judge Hedges or Sam Hauser. And as long as you're writing all this down, include the names of Truman Everts, Walter Trumbull, Warren Gillette, Benjamin Stickney, and Jake Smith."

The names meant nothing to Gabe, but the number of men was important. He could hear the reporter's pencil scratching on paper. Then Mr. Langford went on, "You may quote me as saying nine of us remain firm in our resolve to authenticate or repudiate the natural wonders of the Upper Yellowstone."

"Just a minute while I take that down," Gerald interrupted.

Authenticate? Repudiate? Gabe scratched his head with his free hand. He didn't know what they meant. No matter. What was important to him was what Jim Bridger had told him: "Langford is the real tobacco chew. Straight as an arrer. He'll do right by you." Bridger's word was law and gospel to Gabe.

"Don't put too much emphasis on the Crow threat," Mr. Langford advised. "In fact, I'm sure all of us would prefer that you limited your story merely to the fact that the expedition will depart tomorrow."

The entire Territory had taken up sides for or against these Helena businessmen who dared explore the headwaters of the Yellowstone. Gerald nodded, but he meant to keep folks reading the newspaper by using such scare headlines as NINE TO DEFY CROW THREAT. BRAVE DANGERS OF RUMORED GEYSER-LAND. WILL THEY SURVIVE?

He looked up. "You don't really believe old Bridger's crazy stories, do you? About a mountain of glass? Or a pool with a fire burning in the bottom of it?" Maybe he could bait Mr. Langford into making some brash statement, something to furnish a really sizzling headline.

Gabe, behind the door, clenched his fists. Why did the reporter continue to badger Mr. Langford? It was just the way people badgered Bridger when the old explorer talked about the Upper Yellowstone. Tensely he waited for Mr. Langford's answer; so much depended on it.

Believe his stories?

"I most certainly do believe them," said Langford. Gabe sagged against the wall with relief. "I believe those stories," he went on, "and the ones about the water spout that shoots higher than a flagpole, and the mountain that roars, and the jewel tree, and even the one about the river that runs cold on top and hot on the bottom. I expect to find all these and more at the headwaters." Gabe found himself feeling better with every word Langford said. "You can't rile me, Gerald. I heard those tales from Old Gabe himself."

"When was that?" asked the reporter.

17

Gabe hoped Mr. Langford would tell the same story Bridger had told him.

"In 1866 Bridger served as a guide for a wagon train company transporting freight and emigrants across the plains to the Montana gold camps. I was superintendent for the company at the Montana terminal in Virginia City. During layovers the old boy spent a good many hours spinning yarns in my office."

That's exactly what Bridger told me, Gabe assured himself.

"Oh, come now, Mr. Langford!" the reporter protested. "You are a sensible businessman. You can't be a federal tax collector and not recognize a lie when it stares you in the face! Bridger has the reputation of being the biggest liar west of the Mississippi."

Anger shot through Gabe. He took a step forward; he'd like to go right in there and punch that reporter in the nose. Then his shoulders drooped and he halted. It was the same old story. Nobody believed Bridger. Nobody except him—and Mr. Langford. Long ago he had learned that he could never fight every man that guffawed at Bridger's stories.

He was glad when Langford brushed aside the reporter's derogatory remarks about the famous pathfinder with "I admit Jim Bridger is a top-notch story teller. But I am as positive today as I was in 1866 that there is some truth underlying every yarn of his."

"Oh, sure," was Gerald's halfhearted agreement. "It's true Bridger knows more about the Rocky Mountains than any man, living or dead. When he swears he saw a lake sixty miles long up there and a three hundred foot waterfall, folks might allow that was gospel truth or pretty near it. But not those other wild tales! I guess you know you're being criticized for leading a party into the wilderness just to prove whether or not Old Gabe was lying through his teeth! Jehoshaphat, man! Chances are you'll never come out of there alive."

Gabe heard a noise. He guessed Mr. Langford had stood up in a rush. He must have banged on his desk before he said sharply, "Gerald, you've gone too far! If this expedition were a wild goose chase, do you think so influential a person as General Washburn, a noted soldier and Surveyor General of the Montana Territory, would accept my invitation to serve as its official leader? What about Judge Hedges and Sam Hauser, the banker? Can you name two more level-headed men in this mining camp? *They* aren't dropping out.

"Can't you see that exploring the Upper Yellowstone is vital to the country's welfare? We've put up with half-truths long enough. People are flooding the West in search of land. We've got to know more the potentialities of this remote region, either as a new area for settlement or a military stronghold." He cleared his throat. "If you value your job, take my advice and publish only the announcement of our departure. Thirty days from now, when we have returned to Helena, I'll give you a story that will lift that bowler hat right off that impudent head of yours!"

Gerald gasped and fled.

Gabe waited until he heard the chair creak as Mr. Langford seated himself. Then he straightened his back and moved to the doorway. "Mr. Langford?"

Nathaniel Langford looked up. "Yes." He saw a tall slim youth whose black hair and high cheekbones testi-

19

fied to Indian blood but whose blue eyes indicated he was part white—a half-breed. "What can I do for you?" He quickly took note of the fringed buckskin suit, pack, and uncommonly fine rifle and smiled. "You don't have to tell me; I can guess. At least fifty boys have begged to join the Yellowstone expedition. I'm sorry, but our packers and cook were signed up weeks ago. I can't help you."

Gabe studied the man he had journeyed so far to meet. This was no pale-faced city man, as Gabe had feared he might be. Langford's face was weathered above his brown beard. He was flat-bellied and looked strong, though Bridger had said Langford was "gettin' on in years—must be thirty-eight or so."

Langford had some bookkeeping to bring up to date before leaving the next morning. He wanted to be free of further interruption. "Don't just stand there, boy," he said kindly. "Run along."

Instead of leaving, Gabe dug into his knife sheath, slipped open the secret pocket, and pulled out the letter. He moved forward silently and dropped it on the desk. Langford unfolded the single sheet and read it. He exclaimed, "This letter is from Jim Bridger! I'd know his scrawl anywhere. He writes you're his foster son."

Gabe threw back his shoulders. "That's right."

Mr. Langford read on. "He wants me to take you with me up the Yellowstone."

Gabe nodded enthusiastically. But Mr. Langford looked as if he didn't believe the letter. Oh, golly, if he didn't—! "Long as Old Gabe couldn't come hisself, he sent me to help you find your way up in thar."

"Yes, so the letter says."

20

Gabe lifted the rifle a bit so Mr. Langford could see it was something extra special for a lad his age to own. "I'm a good hunter," he said solemnly.

If Langford heard, he wasn't impressed. "The old boy doesn't mention your name."

"It's Kirkpatrick." He could see that the letter had really flabbergasted Mr. Langford. He just had to believe it. He just had to take him on the expedition.

"Well, I'll have to know more about you. Slip off that pack and sit down."

Gabe eyed the chair beside the desk. He wasn't used to chairs. He had been raised in a tepee and was accustomed to sitting on mats and buffalo robes. But he slipped the pack to the floor and sat down gingerly, the rifle across his knees. Jim Bridger had told him to mind his manners, and the one thing his heart was set on, even if Mr. Langford refused to take him along and he had to *stalk* the explorers, was to make his way up the Yellowstone. He couldn't go in there alone and survive, as he had thought he could. Bridger had impressed him with that fact.

Gabe said his name was George Kirkpatrick and his father had been Andy Kirkpatrick, a free trapper who had traded his pelts at Jim Bridger's post in southwestern Wyoming. His mother was a Shoshone and a cousin to Bridger's wife.

"Pa thought Bridger was the greatest man in the world. And he was. I don't care how folks laugh at him. He could trap and scout better than any mountain man, before he got too old. And he's no liar! I aim to prove that by going up in thar and see for myself that he ain't lied about the Yellowstone."

Langford pursed his lips. The lad certainly was on the

defensive about his foster father. "What about your own father? I mean, why does Bridger describe you as his foster son?"

"The Crows got Pa when I was ten. My mother and the young 'uns died of smallpox. Jim took me in. I helped around the post until he made me go to the mission school. He said my Pa could read and write and would want me lettered." The words ceased abruptly, like a pump gone dry.

"How long were you at the school?"

Gabe squirmed on the hard chair seat. "I didn't stay. I got no use to read and write. Huntin' is all the life I want."

"Oh," Mr. Langford murmured. The boy's aversion to school was understandable. "You preferred living with the Shoshones."

That's not so, Gabe wanted to say, but couldn't, out of loyalty to his mother's people. Actually he disliked the squalor of an Indian camp. He was very proud of his white father, and he didn't want to be all Indian. Yet he had hated the white man's school. He didn't like the smell and racket of cities, and he had ended up feeling that there was no proper place in the world where a half-breed could fit.

He knew how to talk like a white man; he knew Shoshone, too. His father had taught him to trap and hunt and take care of himself in the woods. Aside from his father the only white person he was close to was Jim Bridger. But the way that big lump in Bridger's throat was growing and his eyes failing, he was pretty sure the old man wouldn't last too many more years.

Langford probed gently for more information. "That's a handsome rifle, George. Did Old Gabe give it to you?"

"No, sir. I won it. First prize in a marksmanship contest in Kansas City. Ain't it a beauty?"

Mr. Langford smiled. "Then you really are a good hunter."

"Sure." He was a little nettled. Couldn't Mr. Langford tell just by looking at him? Who but a top sharpshooter would have a new .44 Winchester Model 1866 with a hand-carved gunstock?

There was something he had better straighten out right now. He did not, he explained, want to be called George. Telling him about Mr. Langford's expedition up the Yellowstone, Old Gabe, as Bridger was called now, had said, "Langford writes he wants me to guide him up in thar. Shucks, he don't need me. I told him in sixty-six how to make it from the bend in the river. Likely he's forgot." The aging pathfinder had tightened his gnarled fingers around his cane. "My scoutin' days is about over. I've a mind to send you. I'll fix a map in your mind you'll not forgit." He had chuckled. "How'd you like to carry on for Old Gabe? You go in thar—you'll see I ain't the liar I'm made out to be." After a moment he had muttered, "Langford, he'll know why I'm sendin' you. None of my boys wants to be mountain men. You do. Looks like you're the one to carry on as Young Gabe."

Young Gabe . . .

"So I answer to Gabe, not George," he concluded.

"Now just one more question, Gabe. How did you come to Montana, on foot or horseback?"

Gabe replied that he had worked his passage on the *Emilie*, a steamboat plying the Missouri between Kansas City and Fort Benton, Montana Territory.

23

"How did you travel the one hundred and forty miles from Fort Benton to Helena?"

"Walked," he answered matter-of-factly. He didn't mention that he had made a forced march of it, with scarcely time to rest and eat, because he was so afraid he would miss Mr. Langford.

Langford leaned back in his chair, and stroked his beard. Of course he would take the lad on the expedition. Bridger had asked the favor. A good hunter was always welcome, providing the lad was really good and not just bragging, the way most boys did. Maybe he won the rifle, maybe not. He ended the suspense for Gabe by saying, "All right, I'll make a place for you in the expedition. You'll have to help with the horses and the camp chores."

Gabe bobbed his head. "I'm a good worker. I—I sure do thank you."

The open ledgers reminded Langford of official duties. However, since the expedition would leave in the morning, he wanted Gabe to have a hearty meal or two and some rest. He pushed back his chair and stood. "I'll take you down to Elwyn Bean. He's our head wrangler and is supplying the mule train. If you help line up the packs for him, he'll fill you up with biscuits and bacon."

Gabe jumped to his feet and shouldered his pack. Now that everything had turned out all right, he let himself think about food. For the past few moments he had wondered if his stomach was stuck to his backbone, but he guessed it hurt because he was so prickly and on edge. He hadn't eaten a good meal since he had left the *Emilie*.

"*Okoshoyope tibi tsic djant!*" he exclaimed in Shoshone. Mr. Langford looked so puzzled that he translated: "Bacon heap good! I'm hungry."

24

II

A Good Hunter

IT WAS Tuesday, August twenty-third, and not yet sunrise. Gabe, waking early in the camp on Trail Creek, slipped out of his blanket roll and hurried the short quarter-mile to the Yellowstone River. From the edge of the aspen grove he struck out across open, sparse grass, careful to step over stones and prickly pear cactus. As his leggings brushed clumps of sagebrush, he breathed deeply of the sharp, spicy scent. The smell of sage always stimulated him, helped clear his mind, and sharpen his senses.

Now that he'd left the others sleeping in their tents, it wasn't very difficult to imagine that he was with a party of hunters being guided by Jim Bridger. No, not guided by Old Gabe. By Young Gabe! Ayeeee! He let out a yell at the thought.

He reached the edge of the ancient glacial flood plain and there, fifty feet below, rushed the swift green waters of the Yellowstone. It looked just as Jim said it did.

The millstone of doubt that had occasionally threatened his hero worship of Bridger was suddenly gone. Not that he wasn't devoted to the old pathfinder; he was. But sometimes he'd had to fight with himself to go on believing in that mountain of glass story or the one about the spring with a fire bubbling in the bottom of it.

The Yellowstone must not disappoint him. It must lead him on and on, with one exciting discovery after another. That's why it was so important to find that this gateway to the Upper Yellowstone was exactly the way Bridger had pictured it.

Directly across the river, about three miles back from the water, soared the saw-toothed, white-seamed Snowy Mountains. Downriver, to his left in the north, looped the big bend. "Many the night I camped on the big bend whar the Yellowstone busts out o' the Snowies and turns east," Bridger had recalled while Gabe sat entranced at his feet. "The ol' redhead, Bill Clark of the Lewis and Clark expedition, he set down thar a spell. I recollect that was in July eighteen-ought-six. And that ol' hoss, John Colter, he found elk thar and buffler thicker than flies on a bowl o' clabber. In ought-eight, that war. Your Pa camped there more'n once."

All of a sudden Gabe hankered to swim in the Yellowstone. He wanted to souse in it, to feel it all around him, running through his hair, splashing in his eyes and ears. He just had to *soak* up the Yellowstone.

He plunged down the graveled bank, shucked his buckskins and moccasins, and waded in. The current almost bowled him over, but he laughed as the water pounded at him. This was mountain water, so icy cold it hurt. It was impossible, however, to swim among the jumbled rocks. Within seconds he was so chilled and shiver-

26

ing that he leaped out. There was no breeze, but the cool breath of morning raised a crop of goose-pimples all over him and set his teeth to chattering. No matter.

As he tugged on his buckskins, he felt happier than he had since he was orphaned. This was the life for him. What he wanted to be was a mountain man. He liked the wide spaces, the big sky, the piney smells of the forests. He liked even the washing in icy water, sleeping on the ground, and living almost exclusively on wild game.

But most important, right now, this journey must prove that he had the courage and endurance and know-how to be a real mountain man. Mr. Langford and his friends had talked about the challenge of the Yellowstone. He couldn't understand what they meant by "challenge"; they were all middle-aged, and the middle-aged didn't know about such things, did they? But it certainly was a challenge for *him*. Lately he'd been thinking about the Yellowstone as if it were some great test, like the ones a Shoshone youth underwent to prove his manhood.

He took several deep breaths and flexed his arms and legs. Then he looked southward up the river with its narrowing valley between the jumbled mountains looming on every side, the barrier that had turned back many a trapper and prospector. He couldn't wait to tackle it. Shivering with excitement he scrambled up the bank. Above the aspen grove where the expedition was camped rose a thin trickle of smoke. Good! The day was under way. Soon they'd be on the road again.

As he raced back toward the camp he noticed trout rising on Trail Creek. Too bad there wasn't time for fishing. In the long purple twilight last evening, after he had unsaddled the horses, unloaded the mules, and cut firewood, he had peeled a willow shoot and tied on a string line and baited a small hook with a snowberry. When Judge Hedges saw him haul a leaping, silver-sided trout from the stream, he had come running with his fancy fishing equipment. "Let me give you a feathered fly," the Judge had offered.

Gabe had eyed all the paraphernalia in the Judge's tackle box and chuckled to himself. "No, thanks, I'll use my own." He couldn't imagine why anyone would lug all that stuff when all around there were natural lures like snowberries and grasshoppers.

These nice businessmen that made up the expedition certainly were strange creatures. Instead of comfortable buckskins they wore what Mr. Langford called third-best wool suits and flannel shirts and brimmed hats, with no cartridge belt or knife sheath. Only two had waist guns; the rest used saddle holsters for their rifles, except one elderly man named Everts, whose eyesight was too poor for any kind of shooting, and *his* pockets were stuffed with books. And the folderol these men carried— tackle, poker chips, canteens, mufflers, mechanical duck calls, rubber sheets, concertinas and mouth organs, pencils and notebooks—even a couple of lanterns. The poor pack horses! Gabe felt he could teach them a thing or two about traveling light. His sack of "possibles" contained an extra pair of moccasins, a stone for sharpening the knife, the wadding to clean his rifle, and a half-coat made from a blanket. The wrangler had furnished him with a saddle, even though he had never used one and didn't like it, and a half-broken pinto which he had named Tibo, the Shoshone word for friend. Not that they were friends this soon. It took time for a horse and man to get to trust each other. The first time Gabe had mounted Tibo, he had bucked and sunfished like a demon, but Gabe had hung on. Who wouldn't, with a saddle horn to grab? Tibo still shied a lot just to show Gabe that he had a mind of his own, but that was all right. A man wanted a horse to be a horse, not a worn-out old hack.

At first Gabe had felt pretty superior to the Judge. Not just because the man was fat in the stomach and his arms were flabby, but because he didn't know the first thing about horses. The Judge had let a trader dupe him into buying a four-legged good-for-nothing, the kind a Shoshone would stake out to fool a horse-thieving Crow. Worse, the Judge didn't even know how to night-hobble a horse, let alone lasso it every time the scoundrel ran off. Gabe was always being called on to do it for him; now he took it upon himself to night-picket all the horses. It saved him a lot of work. The others took this favor for granted, but the Judge always thanked him, saying, "Much obliged, son."

Son . . . he hadn't heard that word in a long time.

It was rather nice, the way the Judge said it. It made you want to do things for him. Maybe it was because Hedges was the father of five children that he knew how to make a lad feel good. Whatever it was, Gabe felt closer to the Judge than to any one else, even Mr. Langford.

Mr. Langford was nice, but maybe being a bachelor made him awkward with a young person. If he talked man-level to Gabe, he was too hearty about it. When he wasn't, he was forever clucking watch-out-for-this or don't-do-that-you'll-get-hurt, until Gabe protested,

29

"Look, Mr. Langford. I been raised in the mountains. I can handle an ax. I won't catch cold if my feet gets wet. I can go hunting without getting lost."

He sighed. Maybe after Mr. Langford knew him better and saw that he really could handle horses and build fires that didn't burn a forest of firewood, like Walter Trumbull's, and bring in more game meat than Jake Smith, he'd see Gabe as Gabe saw himself—a mighty capable mountain-man-in-the-making.

He was no greenhorn like white-faced Walter Trumbull, always looking back over his shoulder as if he was afraid something might pounce on him. Gabe looked back often, as Bridger had taught him to, but to memorize the country coming *and* going.

He was no greenhorn either like that Jake Smith, a bandy-legged, crow-voiced fellow whose hair stuck out like bunch grass under his black slouch hat. Jake clumped around in half-length boots, and in the morning when it was chilly he wore a black frock coat over his blue shirt with the celluloid collar. He talked a lot, in between cracking jokes and bragging about what a great hunter he was. Before long Gabe had decided Jake'd be the burr in his blankets this trip.

Every night when camp was being set up Gabe had a thousand things to do, so he couldn't go off hunting. He didn't mind these chores; he'd expected to do them, but during the day he wanted to be free to hunt on his own. He wasn't allowed to. He was made to ride with two or three others, so when a deer or antelope was flushed everybody banged away, and he never got credit for making a kill. He was sure—more than that, he was positive—it was his shots that hit the mark. But Jake always claimed

30

it was *his* kill and insisted he was the only hunter worth the powder to fire a shot. The others paid no attention to Jake. They just laughed. They didn't care whose shot counted, just so there was meat aplenty for supper.

But Gabe really did care. A good hunter always cared. He frowned as he strode toward the campsite. Hunting was the thing he could do better than any of the others— or at least as well. He wondered what they'd say if they had heard Jim Bridger tell him, "Likely thet bunch o' greenhorns can't hit a mountain broadside. You keep 'em in meat, young feller." There was another thing: being *the* hunter would make him feel that he was doing his part. He guessed he'd have to wait for the chance to make a spectacular shot, the kind that would make that Jake Smith's eyes pop out.

Now the smoke from the cookfires had more body. He loped toward where the kitchen tarp was strung between the trees. Nute, the cook, a Negro not much older than Gabe, had the morning meal under way. He wore wool trousers and shirt, boots, and a knitted red cap, even though it was mid-August. "Morning," Nute greeted him. Booby, Nute's black Labrador pup, hurled himself joyously against Gabe, trying to lick his face with a slobbery tongue.

"Morning," Gabe answered brightly, although Shoshones never greeted each other that way. They thought it rude and insulting to a man's intelligence to point out that morning had arrived. But Nute's way was so friendly that Gabe had adopted it.

Nute was shoving sticks in the trench fire over which he had set the iron grates to support the kettles and skillets. "You mind toting the coffee water?" he asked.

31

Gabe picked up the blackened two-gallon pot and hurried to the creek. Booby frolicked along beside him, ears and big paws flapping as he bounded over the sagebrush. Funny to have a dog for a friend. Gabe's father never let him own one because a dog would bother his traps, and in the Shoshone village dogs made good stew when other meat was scarce.

As Gabe returned with the water he saw Lieutenant Doane and five other soldiers crawl out of their tents. Gabe grinned to himself. Jim Bridger never slept under a tent. And neither would he!

He had been disturbed the day before when the six-man military escort from Company F, Second Cavalry, Fort Ellis, had joined the expedition. "Are they coming with us?" he had demanded of Nute. In the Shoshone village he had learned only contempt for the bluecoats.

Nute had nodded.

"Why?"

The Negro explained a little uncomfortably, "For protection."

"Protection? From what?" Bridger hadn't needed protection, ever. He had trapped through the mountains with fewer men in his fur brigades than there were in the whole expedition.

The soldiers were to protect the civilians from the rampaging Crows. But Nute said instead, "We got a general heading this expedition. Generals don't go nowheres without an escort."

After he had thought about it, Gabe simmered down. Maybe a general was like a chief, and of course a chief never went anywhere without a few warriors attending him. Then he got over his immediate dislike of General

Washburn, which had been based solely on the man's being a soldier, after Nute assured him that Washburn had been a big fighter in the war to free the Negroes from slavery and had never, absolutely never, harmed a single Indian. It was certainly hard, when you'd been raised with the Indians for most of your life, to try and do things and see things like white men.

He put the coffeepot on the fire. While Nute was up to his elbows in flour making biscuits, Gabe cut off thick ham slices and dropped them in the skillets. Then he opened the fifty-pound sack of coffee beans. Nute had showed him how to set up the coffee grinder on a tree stump. The racket he made grinding the beans woke the others. As Gabe cranked the handle and the grounds dribbled into the catch drawer he saw Mr. Langford step from his tent, followed by Judge Hedges, General Washburn, and a Mr. Sam Hauser, a banker—whatever a banker was. All wore gray undershirts, their trousers single-buttoned at the waist, suspenders hanging slack. Suspenders. Ayeeee! How grand it would be to have bright red straps with glistening buckles to hold up your leggings.

The General led the parade to the creek, his wash kit in hand. Being used to grizzled trappers, Gabe couldn't get over the way the General shaved his cheeks every morning and brushed his small pointed beard. Then Hauser dropped his undershirt, knelt, and started splashing like a buffalo. Gabe respected the banker because he looked so fierce. His whiskers bristled like a porcupine's. He had a hawklike nose and swore a lot, but never at anyone in particular.

Gabe decided he had ground enough coffee. He pulled out the drawer and dumped the contents in the pot. Then he turned the ham slices, which were good and black on the under side. "Have I got time to saddle up a few horses?" he asked Nute. The answer was yes. Since each of the gentlemen had his own saddle horse and pack horse, this took a bit of doing, particularly when you were anxious to be on the way, as Gabe was. None of the businessmen looked after their horses; they just rode them and left the rest to Gabe.

The wrangler and his helper took care of the mules and loaded them, since this was a very special skill which Gabe had not learned. He was used to saddlebags, or parfleches. The soldiers had their own mess and rations and tended their own mounts. Gabe could understand the businessmen and soldiers camping separately. In a fur brigade, partners gathered together around separate fires, but he couldn't figure why there was no joking back and forth between the civilians and soldiers and why they didn't gather around one big campfire after dark and swap stories and sing.

No matter. He shrugged. New friends, new ways.

After a bit he returned and pulled the skillets off the fire.

Nute meantime had scrambled the eggs. He wrapped his hand in a towel and lifted a pan of golden brown biscuits from the portable oven. "Ham done? Coffee boiled good?" When Gabe nodded, Nute banged on the dishpan with his iron spoon and shouted, "Co-ome and get it!"

The wranglers loaded their plates first and ate hurriedly. They would strike the tents and rope the tarps on the pack saddles while the gentlemen breakfasted. The latter served themselves scrambled eggs, flapjacks, fried trout, and Nute's feather-light biscuits, but passed up the shriveled, blackened meat. But Jake, who never missed a chance to wisecrack about something, forked a piece and held it high. "What's this? Cremated cedar bark? Nute, did you fry the General's boots by mistake?"

Nute chuckled and shook his head.

Gabe spoke up. "I cooked the ham."

"You call this ham?" Jake jeered.

To stop Jake from teasing Gabe, Judge Hedges called out, "Last one through breakfast scours the pots!" Jake was no worker, he liked to stand around telling jokes while others cut the firewood and pounded in the tent stakes. He forgot about the ham and started bolting his food.

Gabe wished there was some way to show everyone, not only Jake, that he was a good hunter and shouldn't have to do squaw work, like cooking. By the time the expedition was ready to move he had a glimmering of an idea, something he had learned from the Shoshones, a real eye-popper. If he could get the chance; Jake's constant brag became tiresome after a few days—especially his brag about what a good hunter he was.

As had been decided previously because of the Crow threat, three or four rode in advance, the remainder accompanied the pack train, and the soldiers formed the rear guard. This morning Gabe, Langford, Hauser, and Jake rode about a half mile ahead of the others. They moved across the valley floor, enjoying the sunshine and the peaks etched sharply against a cloudless sky. As they neared a stand of cottonwood or willow, finches, redpolls, and chickadees exploded from the branches. Large flocks of blackbirds soared in shrill flight, like buckshot scatter-

35

ing high and dropping away on every side, then swooped back to the ground where they strutted brazenly, feathers glittering iridescent green and purple, screeching their harsh notes.

At midmorning the advance riders flushed four antelope. The fleet animals rose on their hind legs, wheeled, and fled in high, bounding leaps. Because Tibo was fractious and still gun shy, Gabe had to ride with his rifle holstered. He had grabbed for it and had it partially withdrawn when Jake, riding on his left, fired right over the pinto's head. Instantly on the far side Langford's and Hauser's guns barked. Tibo reared violently and pitched Gabe and rifle to the ground. Hauser grabbed the reins and fought the terrified pinto to a standstill, so Gabe would not be trampled.

Langford dismounted and ran to him. In the few minutes it took Gabe to recover, Langford's hands tested arms and legs for broken bones. He asked anxiously, "Gabe, are you hurt?" Gabe got to his feet and said disgustedly, "No!" His first thought was for the rifle. He picked it up, wiped it off carefully, and examined it to see if the sights were damaged. All this time Jake was crowing about having shot one of the antelope. Then he said, without sounding the least bit sorry, "Better luck next time, Injun."

Gabe was furious. He hated being called "Injun." He was humiliated at being thrown. And the good chance he'd been waiting for, to prove his marksmanship, had been ruined by Jake's unsportsmanlike shot. Legs spraddled, blue eyes blazing, he cried out, "I could have kilt two antelope if you hadn't fired right over my horse's head."

Jake began to laugh, but Hauser snapped, "Jake!" The little man sobered. "Aw, I didn't mean nothin'. That's the trouble with these dumb Injuns, they can't take a joke."

Langford said sharply, "Gabe is no dumb Injun. Don't let me hear you call him that again. And after this, watch where you place your shots."

"What's everybody so het up for?" Jake complained. "I said I didn't mean anything. Sorry, Gabe. Better luck next time. How about dressing out my antelope for me?"

"A *good* hunter dresses out his own animal," Gabe answered stiffly and remounted. The pinto was still quivering, so he stroked the little horse's neck.

Hauser chuckled. He nodded to Langford and Gabe and said, "Let's go!" The three rode on.

By midday Gabe had decided on a plan. Instead of lolling on the grass with the others, while the horses grazed, he waited until Mr. Langford and his friends were dozing. Then he led Tibo to the edge of the riverbank and down a game trail to the bottomland. It was a mile wide here, gravelly and covered intermittently with cottonwood and osier dogwood. He knew the wranglers and the two soldiers standing guard had watched him leave, but they wouldn't call him back.

At the bottom, for a quarter of an hour, he ran the pinto back and forth to get him used to the brush and rocks so he wouldn't shy so much. Then he toed hard on the horse's flanks, put him to a gallop, checked him one-handed as he unholstered the rifle speedily, and pulled back on the hammer. Tibo's ears flicked back and forth. He danced sideways. Because of the pressure on the reins, he couldn't rear. Gabe purposely had no shells in the

37

magazine; he didn't want the others to come running if they heard shots.

Over and over he repeated the riding, checking, and unholstering. Now Tibo was used to the sound of the rifle being whipped out of the leather saddle holster and didn't toss his head when the hammer and trigger clicked. Gabe kept at it until Tibo stopped and remained absolutely still while he leaped from the saddle. Finally he was satisfied. He rode to the river's edge and let the stocky, tough little horse drink. Tibo was smart and getting used to Gabe. He wouldn't have traded the little beast for any of those rocking-chair nags up above.

Mr. Langford rode a handsome roan stallion, and the General had a high-stepping mare that might look fine on a parade ground, but whether or not she would hold up on a mountain trail remained to be seen.

Gabe got back just as the expedition was starting again and once more rode up ahead with Langford, Hauser, and Jake. The pack train had to hold to the pace that was best for the heavily laden mules.

"Strange we don't see more game," Langford mentioned later in the afternoon. "I guess it's ham and beans for supper."

"You won't have ham if Gabe cooks it," Jake joked.

Gabe didn't say anything. He looked straight ahead, praying hard for the chance that would put old frock coat Jake in his place once and for all. Just one *good* chance.

"If we do raise something, Gabe gets the first shot," Hauser told Jake.

Gabe flicked a glance at the little man. Jake didn't like the idea at all; he looked as though he'd eaten green chokecherries. Now I have to prove myself, Gabe worried. Elk; if only he could spot elk. Elk! Not just a deer or antelope, but real game. Now that the west side of the valley was in the shadow of the ridge, this time of year elk—*padahia*, the Shoshones called them—spent the hot daylight hours in the high meadows and did not come down to water until toward evening when cooling mist began to gather over the river bottom. If only the elk had started to drift down out of the timber toward the river.

He tensed as he rode and looked in every direction for the telltale blur of brown and tan in the thickets. Easing his feet back in the stirrups so his heels were free, he rode with his right hand resting lightly on the rifle.

Then he saw them! Two elk were traveling purposefully toward the river, handsome, tossing their antlers, rising gracefully over brush and boulders in their path. Gabe spurred the pinto and shortened the distance between him and them; the wind from upriver was in his favor. Just as the elk saw him he checked Tibo, kicked free of the stirrups, swung his leg over the saddle as he unholstered the Winchester, and dropped lightly to the ground. As the elk wheeled, he ran ahead of Tibo. Then he stopped, aimed, and fired.

One animal went down; the other bounded off through the brush. Too bad. If he could have fired from the saddle he was sure he could have hit the two.

The others rode up, leading Tibo. Jake was flushed with anger and his eyes looked hot. Langford didn't try to hide his astonishment. "What a crack shot you are!" he complimented Gabe.

After a quick look at Jake, Hauser said, "Now we know who is the best hunter in this expedition, eh Langford?"

He leaned over and pumped Gabe's hand. "Well done, lad. Ve-ry well done."

Gabe was grinning so hard that his face was creased from ear to ear. He wanted to shout and brag, the way a Shoshone did after a spectacular shot, but he fought down the impulse. He didn't want to sound like Jake. So he drew his knife and said as nonchalantly as he could, "Elk steaks will sure taste mighty good for a change."

III

Crow Signals!

THE next morning, mindful of the Crow threat, General Washburn ordered all men to escort the pack train. Knowing the expedition tents, blankets, food and ammunition were rich plunder, he wanted a strong guard to protect the supplies. The plan was to hold to the west bank of the Yellowstone until the reported "grand canyon" and falls were reached.

Gabe rode midway along the line on the side nearest the river so he could get a glimpse now and then of the hurrying stream. He was looking for the yellow rock, or stone, for which the river was named. So far he had seen none. Did the very early French trappers who had named it the *Roche Jaune*—Yellow Rock—mean this portion here where the banks were a light buckskin yellow? Or was it *Mi tsi a di zi*, as the very old Minnetarees called it in their guttural Siouan tongue, a river where the banks were as yellow as the meadowlark's breast? It didn't matter—light or dark, as long as it was really yellow, not a

41

sort of squaw yellow like this part, but the yellow a warrior would paint on his shield.

Gabe always felt good in the early morning, his favorite time of day. The sky was cloudless, and once the low-lying mist had evaporated the atmosphere was crystal clear. The mountains stood out in bold relief, each pine and spruce distinct on the timbered flanks, the rock crevices etched sharply on the barren granite girdle, the peaks glittering. His nose wrinkled. When there was no wind to sweep away all but the penetrating scents of evergreen and sage, he could catch the underlying fragrance of ripening wild gooseberry, pungent willow and fireweed, and dew-wet grass. He was glad to see the valley gradually pinching in, the floor steepening. On the west side the foothills of gray and brown rock streaked with white marled clay were stubbled with scrub cedar and juniper. A few humpbacked ridges dribbled out to the very riverbank. The horses and mules held a steady pace over the first few of these gentle inclines, but ahead they would have to climb one hill after another.

Unconsciously he pressed forward in the saddle. That's where he wanted to be—way up there. Bridger had told him, "The part you got your sights on is south of the Gardner River. You'll cross it. But I ain't tellin' a sharp boy like you whar the boundary be. I mean, between the outside world and what's in thar." The old pathfinder had chuckled. "You'll *know*, I'm thinkin'. Least a young feller who's looking to be a mountain man ought to know. City folks now, they'll likely miss it. But the likes of you 'n' me—" His voice trailed off, leaving Gabe with a thousand questions unanswered.

He couldn't wait to cross the Gardner River. They

42

should reach it today or tomorrow, if nothing delayed the expedition. With everything going along so well—pretty well anyhow—there should be no trouble. The only thing that bothered him a little was that the city men weren't obeying the General's orders.

For instance, this morning when the General had assigned Jake to ride midway the length of the pack train, Jake had stirred up an argument. Bold as a magpie, he had said, "I ain't ridin' nowheres but up in front. Let some one else eat dust. Get one of the soldiers. They have to do what you say."

"And you don't have to?" Washburn questioned him coldly. As the official leader, he was giving the orders and expected to see them carried out. He rode in the lead, as if he were on parade, every inch the military, wearing polished boots, gauntlets, and a slouch-brimmed hat.

"You're darn tootin', I don't," Jake answered. "None of us businessmen has to follow orders. We're civilians. We're paying our own way. It'd be different if this was a government survey party or a genuine military expedition, but it ain't."

"Orders or not," Hauser interrupted in his blunt way, "you'll guard the pack train if that's what Washburn thinks necessary. Who in blazes cares if he has to take orders now and then? Cooperate!" He glared at Jake.

Gabe held his breath. Was a fight brewing? Would the men take sides?

"I'm afraid Jake has a point," remarked Warren Gillette. Benjamin Stickney, an inseparable companion of Gillette's, chimed in, "I agree. We don't have to take orders. But that's not to say we won't rally round when necessary, General, or will neglect our share of guard duty."

43

He smiled and even dared to josh Washburn. "Don't be such a bear for discipline among your friends."

Mr. Everts, who was more of a listener than a talker, tilted his head back so he could see better through the glasses pinched on the bridge of his nose. "I'll ride in Jake's place. Glad to." Over fifty and half-blind, Everts was never overanxious to be in front.

Gabe thought the General should have more support than that of the elderly Mr. Everts. "I'll ride midway on the side next to the river," he volunteered. He could see that the General was having to struggle to control his temper.

Mr. Langford, quick to salve any ill feeling, pointed out, "You all agreed to have Washburn as our leader. As such he has a right to expect friendly cooperation from all of us. He has our safety uppermost in his mind. After all, this is Crow country."

Everyone seemed agreeable now, even Jake, as long as he could ride up in front. The expedition strung out along the riverbank and advanced a few miles in orderly fashion. But later, Gabe observed, looking back, Gillette and Stickney and Trumbull peeled off and pursued some antelope until they were a good mile to the west of the company and close to the timber. He frowned, and watched them anxiously. There could be Crows lying in wait behind the big trees. But the three came straggling back, and, Gabe noticed with considerable satisfaction, without any antelope.

Then Mr. Everts rode close enough to the bushes so that even he could see they were loaded with black cherries and paused to fill his hat. And the Judge, who'd been studying the river closely, stopped to fish the rapids. Gabe

44

wanted badly to ride back and tell the Judge and Mr. Everts that if they dropped too far behind they were practically begging the Crows to waylay them. But he didn't; they should know what they were doing, and his job was to stay midway down the pack train and be on guard. After all, this *was* Crow country! And the Crows were on the warpath. They probably had lookouts atop the mountains to watch the progress of the expedition. He'd be willing to bet that the Crows were waiting for them to get boxed in in some tight spot, and then, when the odds were all in their favor, they would attack.

The possibility made his scalp prickle.

A flock of geese wheeled overhead. If only he'd brought his father's shotgun; the Winchester was too heavy for bird shooting. Suddenly, shots rang out. Tibo shied, but not so badly that Gabe couldn't see Jake shooting right over the heads of the pack mules. They tried to stampede, but being roped together, could only kick and stumble and break for the riverbank. Gabe and a few others grabbed the bridles to keep the whole string from plummeting over the steep bluff. Even before the dust settled and the mules were straightened out, the wrangler started cursing Jake fiercely. But Jake just laughed. "I got a goose, didn't I?" he bragged.

At midday Gabe was glad to hear the General tell Nute that they would not be dallying long for lunch. "So fix us some coffee and cold biscuit and tinned peaches," the General instructed. And you could tell, too, by the changed tone of the General's voice that he had decided not to be the military type of leader. But all the same he intended to be boss.

While Gabe made the rounds with the coffeepot he

45

heard Washburn trying to impress on his friends the necessity for vigilance and caution. Gillette and Stickney and Trumbull all were so sure there wasn't any real danger. They hadn't seen the least sign of Crows in the vicinity. Besides, they reasoned, the expedition was large, well-armed, and possessed plenty of reserve ammunition.

"I bet we could stand off two hundred and fifty Crows," Gillette averred.

Gabe wondered whether Gillette had ever fought any Crows.

"What good are guns if I'm the only good shot, and the rest of you can't shoot worth sour apples?" Jake spoke out. "I bet I'm the only one, excepting the soldiers, and maybe Gabe, who could hit a target at twenty yards with a revolver. It's the quick shot from the hip, without having to get set, that counts in Indian warfare."

Langford hooted. "What do you know about fighting Indians? By the time you came out to the Territory in a stagecoach the Indians were no trouble."

Jake was right, or partly so, but Gabe kept his mouth shut; this was a problem for the leaders. Nobody was asking for his opinion, though he well knew how the Crows would stalk a party for days maybe and then, after dark, close in to massacre the sleeping men. *That* was when a quick shot from the hip could really count.

"I still say," Jake spoke around a mouthful of biscuit, "that not one of you could hit my hat at twenty yards with a revolver."

Hauser chewed his biscuit, then whipped out his waist gun and aimed at Jake's hat. "Want me to try?" he challenged, laughing.

Jake tore the hat off his head. When the others laughed

at him for sneaking out on a bet, a crafty grin spread over his face. He loped to a tree stump, plumped the hat on it, and said, "All right, prove it! But it will cost you two bits a shot. That's a brand new hat."

Within a few minutes the whole group was blazing away at the hat. At first Jake covered his face and wouldn't look at it. But when he peered between his fingers and saw shot after shot missing it, he began taunting the poor marksmen. The more coins he pocketed, the louder he jeered.

Gabe, on the sidelines, saw Mr. Langford pick up his small-bore rifle, and slip off behind a gooseberry bush. A few seconds later he fired, riddling the hat.

"Somebody ruined my hat!" Jake yelled, and ran forward to rescue it. The others doubled up with laughter. But Gabe didn't laugh. It was depressing and sort of scary, too, to realize that not a single one of those men, other than Jake, *was* a good shot. He hoped the expedition didn't run into any Crows!

Not more than an hour later, when the General and Langford, out in front, turned away from the riverbank to avoid a thick stand of cottonwoods, Washburn signaled the riders to come forward. "Look!" he shouted, pointing to the ground. "Indian tracks!"

Gabe saw the imprints of moccasins and unshod ponies and a dozen parallel grooves, such as could be worn by the poles of Indian travois, the crude rawhide stretchers lashed behind ponies and used for carrying skins for their lodges. The sign, as he read it, was at least two days old. It indicated that a hunting party had passed leisurely, not a war party. Probably they had been the inhabitants of a small village, because there were footprints of squaws and children in the dust. This was something to consider but nothing to cause real alarm.

Langford, alongside him, was saying to Hauser and the General, "Doesn't look like fresh sign to me."

Hauser pulled on his long nose and added, "I don't think a war party would be traveling with squaws and travois." When Lieutenant Doane joined them and was consulted because he was an experienced Indian fighter, he said, "I'd guess that, judging by the litter they've dropped, a small band went through here on a hunt."

"What do you think, Gabe?" Langford asked.

"I didn't know you could read sign so good," Gabe blurted and then looked down. That was no way to compliment his friends. "You're right," he added, pleased to be asked his opinion.

But Jake and his friends were riding around excitedly, pointing to this imprint and that one and alarming the others, until Jake got so worked up he shouted, "Don't just squat here like ducks in a barrel! Everybody turn around! Head back to Fort Ellis. And hurry, before we're attacked!" He rode pell-mell at the General, reined up sharply, and demanded, "Do something! You're the leader; start giving orders!"

Washburn sucked in his cheeks to keep from laughing and managed to say with feigned surprise, "But Jake, you made it clear you would not obey orders, so why should I bother to issue them?"

Gabe pressed his hand over his mouth to hide a delighted grin. Good for Washburn!

Jake's cheeks flamed. "This is different. Our lives are in danger." He waved his right arm. "Follow me, boys. I'll lead the way back to the fort."

It looked as though the expedition might break up here and now. But Washburn said crisply, "Panic will get us nowhere. The lieutenant is an experienced Indian fighter, and when he says we're in no immediate danger and is backed up by Langford and Hauser, and even Gabe, it would be folly for us to scatter like chickens. This is not the time to disperse what strength we have."

"I demand—" Jake began, but Judge Hedges cut in swiftly, "Gabe, isn't there some story about the Crows staying out of the headwaters country? That they think it's the home of evil spirits?"

Everyone looked at Gabe. What could he say that would keep the expedition moving on up the river?

"I never knowed the Crows to hunt south of the Gardner River, and that's only a few miles from here. Once we get past it, we shouldn't have no trouble. The old trail turns west somewheres up ahead; the old trail used by the Indians, I mean. It crosses a pass and then drops down into the Madison Valley. It don't hold to the river, south, the way we're going." To make sure there would be no turning back, he offered, "General, I'll scout ahead, if you'll let me. I mean, if it will help. If I can prove the Indians have turned off to the west, you'll know they aren't going to attack us, won't you?"

"Some advance scouting is absolutely essential," Washburn decided, so Hauser and Langford immediately volunteered to accompany Gabe.

"I demand a vote!" Jake objected. "All in favor of returning to Fort Ellis say 'aye.'" When no one supported him, he blustered, "We'll take another vote after the scouts report back."

Gabe let out a big sigh of relief. The pack train once

49

more got under way with the General, Hedges, Everts, Lt. Doane, and Jake in the lead. Gillette, Stickney, and Trumbull rode midway, the wranglers and Nute and Booby at the rear of the pack animals, and behind them, the military escort. Gabe, Hauser, and Langford spurred their horses and soon left the others far behind.

They saw nothing more suspicious than the usual grassland and cottonwood stands, and as Gabe had said, about ten miles farther up the river the trail did indeed turn west. There was ample evidence that the Indians had gone that way, but as a precaution Hauser suggested they scout the left fork, or river route, for several miles. As they were riding along, he asked Gabe, "Is that story true about the Indians? That they avoid the headwaters country because they are afraid of evil spirits?"

"Partly." Gabe nodded. "The Shoshones, the Bannocks, the Crows—they camped and fished by the lake, but their trails went *around* the headwaters, not through the heart of them. There's one place in thar," he said, quoting Jim Bridger, "where the ground smokes something fierce and the air is poisonous and—" He shivered, remembering the weird tales he had heard from the Shoshone medicine man. Then, afraid that if he painted too lurid and frightening a picture Hauser and Langford might want to turn back, he added hastily, "But it's a secret place. We wouldn't have to go thar."

Langford said, "Gabe, I know you like to say *thar* because that's the way Bridger and the mountain men say it. And I know you want to be just like Bridger. But it's far more important to be yourself. You don't want to be an imitation of the real thing, now do you?"

Gabe bridled. He didn't intend to be an imitation; he

50

was going to be a real mountain man. "Bridger's good enough for me." He bristled defensively.

But, Langford pointed out, Bridger's day was over. The day of the fur brigade was long since past. In another five or ten years there would be no need for pathfinders or scouts.

Gabe had heard Bridger say the same thing. He'd thought about it sometimes, wondering what it would be like to be a mountain man in a world that didn't need men like that. "How can I be myself," he blurted, "when I don't know what myself is?"

Hauser assured him, "You've plenty of time to find yourself. I think what friend Langford was trying to say was that you are a fine lad and should strive to be the kind of man you want to be and not copy someone else. Maybe this trip will help answer some of your questions."

"I sure hope so," Gabe answered. He added slowly, "All right, I won't say *thar* any more."

The three discovered no Indian sign on the river trail, nor any new sign on their return to the campsite, which was directly opposite the massive thrust of Emigrant Peak and set back a few yards from a little creek. The men came running to hear their report. Hauser gave it, concluding, "So there's no reason for alarm."

To be fair, the General asked Jake, "Do you want a vote on whether or not we return to Fort Ellis?"

"No." Jake spat deliberately. "But if we see any more Crow sign, I'll sure ask for one."

Maybe there was no reason for alarm, but there certainly was need for caution. They were still a good jump from the Gardner. Gabe was thankful there was no further talk of turning back and hoped nothing more would happen to stir Jake up. Maybe the scare was for the best, if it made the travelers more aware of the Crow threat.

The General set up a schedule for night guard duty. With the campfire as the center point, two soldiers were to patrol a half circle to the south from ten P.M. to one A.M. and be relieved by two more from one A.M. to five A.M. The civilians would also pair off and patrol the radial area five hundred paces to the north. Mr. Langford and the Judge offered to stand the first watch and Washburn and hawk-nosed Hauser the second.

Gabe was a little disappointed. He was just itching to stand guard. He'd heard his father and Bridger talk about it so much, about what a test of a man's courage and steadiness it was. But he guessed he would have to be patient and wait his turn.

After supper and chores, Gabe fixed his night spot. He cleared a bit of ground and dug a slight hollow for his hips. Then he laid out his blankets, checked the rifle to see that it was loaded, and laid it *just so*, where he could if necessary place his hand on the trigger in a second's time. He was glad he didn't have to bother with undressing and wearing a nightshirt, like the others. In fine weather like this he wouldn't want to sleep under a tent either; the stars were cover enough. Later on he might waken and feel as if there were a cold knife biting into his neck and ribs, or his face and hair might be clammy with dew because he had threshed around in his sleep until his covers came loose. But that was nothing. All a fellow had to do was burrow under the blankets, and pull the edges as tight and warm as a cocoon, and drift off to sleep again. And if you were bedded down in sagebrush, as he was tonight, or in a forest of evergreens, you could always smell the sage or pine through the musty wool of the blanket.

At first he lay quietly, his head propped on his arms, watching the men. The soldiers were gathered around their own campfire, smoking and drinking coffee. The wranglers were sleeping one-ear-awake beside the rope and brush corral they had built to hold the horses and mules. He could hear the animals feeding on the bunch grass. When they stood motionless, heads up, staring toward the fire, their eyes blazed like giant fireflies. He wondered if Nute were sleeping with Booby snuggled against his back. The first night he had put his blankets alongside Nute's, and Booby had wriggled between them. After an hour, Gabe had to get up, shake his blankets and even his clothing, and move to another spot! The fleas had nearly driven him crazy.

Mr. Langford sat on a sack of beans, writing in his journal. At least that's what he called it, a day-to-day journal of the weather, and how far they had traveled, and what they had for supper, and what the country looked like. Was he writing anything tonight about the Indian scare? Judge Hedges, Hauser, and the General were also writing in their journals—and Lieutenant Doane too, he noticed, craning his neck to see. This was certainly the writingest bunch! The others were discussing something called a Franco-Prussian War. Mr. Everts, as usual, was trying to read a book by firelight, but every time he bent over the book his glasses fell off. Pretty soon everyone started yawning and drifting toward the tents, all except Langford and the Judge, who were to stand the first guard.

Gabe yawned and gave up trying to keep his eyes open.

But he wakened later to see Langford and Hedges building up the campfire and warming the leftover coffee. After a bit they resumed their patrol, Langford moving quietly in the direction of the river, the Judge in the opposite direction. Gabe just ached to prowl around in the dark, too. He wanted to find out whether or not, as his Pa had said, the hours of night guard duty in Indian country were the longest, loneliest, *prickliest* hours in a man's life. He wished he had been paired off with Mr. Langford. The Judge was too—well, he was old and needed his sleep. Besides he didn't know anything about Crow tactics. It was only right that the younger men take over guard duty. In a few moments Gabe had convinced himself that the Judge was in danger, so he squirmed out of his blanket roll, checked on his knife, and set out to trail the Judge. The Judge needed protecting, he really did. The way he was plodding heavy-footed over the ground he was easy prey for any sneaky Crow!

When Hedges turned to pace back toward camp, Gabe decided to swing to the north and then over to the river. Was he a good enough stalker to locate Mr. Langford in the dark and get real close without being discovered? Keeping his hand on the knife sheath, moving cautiously around the clumps of sagebrush and wild gooseberry that loomed darkly under starlight, he moved far away from the campfire. Now he could see only its reflection and a few infrequent sparks rocketing skyward. He frowned. That fire wasn't a good idea. If Crow lookouts saw it, they would know exactly where the expedition was camped! For a moment he wavered between returning to camp and putting out the fire, and finding Mr. Langford and getting up nerve enough to tell him to do it.

It would be best to talk to Mr. Langford first; he turned east toward the river. The towering thrust of Emigrant Peak loomed black against the sky. A few moments later he thought he heard something moving on his right. He dropped behind a clump of sagebrush and waited breathlessly, staring hard until his eyes watered, listening until his ears ached. Soon he saw a dark shadow outlined against the stars. Whew! It was only Mr. Langford!

At the same time, however, his attention was drawn to a fire flaring high on the slope of Emigrant Peak. At first he thought the fire might be a lightning-set smudge coming to life. Then he remembered there had been no storms since leaving Helena. He watched apprehensively as the fire soared in a brilliant pillar of flame. He jumped up, meaning to call Mr. Langford to look at it, but glancing southward he saw another fire blaze on a high point. Smothering a cry, he wheeled around to the north. Atop the Trail Creek pass through which the expedition entered the Yellowstone Valley, a third fire flickered and soared. Crow signal fires!

The fire the Judge had built up had revealed the location of the expedition!

"Signal fires!" he shouted in Langford's direction and raced to put out the campfire. He heard Langford answer and start yelling to rouse the camp.

As they raced for buckets and kettles, Gabe saw the men burst from the tents, Everts in nightcap and nightshirt and fumbling for his glasses, the others frantically pulling on trousers and boots.

He filled the buckets and raced to the fire just in time to hear Jake yelling, "Get your guns! Shoot! Shoot!"

"No! No!" Gabe shouted. "You might hit Judge

Hedges! He's out there somewhere!" He hurled water on the flames and jumped back as the steam and smoke billowed over him. Meantime General Washburn was bawling orders and had the men take defensive positions behind the tents by the pile of saddles. They were told to hold fire until he ordered an attack.

Gabe raced to pick up his rifle; he strapped on his cartridge belt and headed out toward the Judge. He met the Judge running toward camp; they both halted where they were and took guard position on the ground, back-to-back. In a few seconds the campsite was dark and absolutely quiet.

Since there was only a slight wind from the west the smallest sound was magnified. Every time a branch of sagebrush rustled Gabe's heart thumped in anticipation. It felt good to have the Judge's warm back against his. Now he could believe that night guard duty in Indian country brought the loneliest, prickliest hours of a man's life. Slowly, oh so slowly, the soft bleaching of night brought the sagebrush into blurred focus. It seemed as though the most welcome words he had ever heard were Washburn's "All clear!"

Gabe rose slowly to his feet, worked the kinks out of his legs, and trailed the Judge to camp. He was worried; he had a hunch what would happen now, and his heart sank as he heard voices clamoring for an immediate return to Fort Ellis. The argument got hotter and hotter. Finally Jake, as expected, demanded that each man vote aloud on whether or not to retreat to the safety of the nearest stockade.

The decision was pretty certain, with everyone so upset, and Gabe didn't care whose turn it was to vote. He shouted, "You can all run for the fort, but I ain't going to! Shucks, if you're travelin' in Indian country, you got to expect *some* trouble. But I aim to see that yellow canyon, even if I got to fight the whole Crow nation single-handed!"

IV

The Secret of the Yellowstone

GABE'S outburst was followed by utter silence. Then Langford supported him by saying, "Before leaving Helena we all understood that we might run into trouble. But we were the nine, remember? who weren't going to allow the Crow threat to keep us from exploring the Yellowstone. I, for one, have no intention of running for home."

"Nor I," chorused Hauser and Hedges.

Washburn seized the initiative. "Those of you who wish to return to Helena are free to do so. You'll be furnished sufficient provisions and ammunition."

Good for him! He had knocked the punch out of Jake's demand.

When no one spoke up for a return, Washburn continued, "The important thing is to move on, under cover of this morning fog." He checked his gold watch.

"Gentlemen, in fifteen minutes we head south. Mr. Bean, strike the tents. Nute, divide up the cold biscuit among us. Gabe, saddle up."

"Yes, *sir*!" Vastly relieved, Gabe leaped to obey. That's what he wanted, action—and in the right direction.

By midmorning he sensed that maybe the Crows might not be the only threat to the progress of the expedition. The weather turned against them. Although the fog lifted partially, dark clouds brooded over the ridges, and the higher peaks were completely hidden. The valley closed in about the river and the ground rose slowly but steadily. When the fine mist had thickened to a steady, cold drizzle, the General called a halt for the men to don jackets and waterproofs. Gabe slipped into his blanket coat, but rode bareheaded; the others had hats, save Everts, who had lost his and now wore a black shawl over his head.

The trail lifted and pitched so much that Gabe began to feel that the Yellowstone was trying to force them to a halt. The mules balked on the stubborn ground, and their packs required continual adjustment; the pace slowed to a crawl. The hogbacks stringing riverward from the west ridge became more numerous, each rise a little steeper and more rocky, until even the saddle horses had to have time to "blow" before tackling a new one.

After a bit Gabe tensed. The expedition was approaching a curve in the trail. Would there be Crows lying in wait, ready to pounce? He unholstered his rifle, as did the others, but no Crows appeared.

Then the cavalcade had to string out single file to pass along a game trail that led through a forest of pine, fir, and spruce, where it was impossible to see more than fifty yards in any direction. Just as Gabe began to wonder if they ever would reach the Gardner, there it was, a swift noisy stream. Tibo fought against entering the water, but Gabe kept toeing him until the little horse struck out for the opposite bank. The Gardner was not deep, but there were treacherous holes in its rocky bed, and the heavily laden mules and pack horses had to be guided carefully to keep them from being swept off their feet.

By midafternoon, after hours of slipping on the rain-slick trail, they came to a small grassy clearing. The General called a halt. Soon the fires were smoking and the tents were up. The riders tended their own horses, and some cut firewood so Gabe and Nute could hurry the supper. The aroma of coffee and the tantalizing smell of the ham and elk steaks and fried potatoes as he turned them made Gabe's mouth water. Nute stirred up a double batch of biscuits and a big pan of gravy. Gabe ate until he was so full he couldn't bend without grunting.

The drizzle turned into a hard rain, and the campsite was so dark that the men went to bed. Mr. Langford tried to insist on Gabe's sleeping in his tent, but not even on a cold rainy night would Gabe consent. However, Mr. Langford looked so determined that Gabe thought he had better compromise. "Somebody has to keep the cook-fire going all night. Nute's tired. I'll do it." That way he would be sleeping under the tarpaulin which the wranglers had strung between the trees to provide protection for the kitchen area and cookfire. The rain drumming on the cloth lulled him to sleep, but he wakened often enough to add wood to the fire. At daylight there was no difficulty in stirring up a hot blaze to cook oatmeal, flap-jacks, and coffee.

"Some outing!" Jake grumbled as he ate. "If the Crows don't get us, pneumonia will."

The mules were so fractious from the cold and rain that the wranglers asked Gabe's help. One little animal gave him a lot of trouble; it shied and nipped as he set the saddle on its back. After the side packs were filled and odd articles balanced on top of these, it bucked everything off into the mud. Four tries later Gabe finally lashed the ropes into some semblance of security. Then the mule ran between two trees and tried to rub off its pack. There it got stuck and brayed loudly. "You can just stay stuck!" Gabe cried. His buckskin leggings were muddied and wet to the knees, and his jacket was clammy cold across his shoulders. Although droplets ran off his forehead into his eyes and down his nose, he tackled another mule. The wranglers were having similar difficulties. By the time the last animal was loaded, the whole string had wound around until the ropes were an exasperating tangle.

Finally the expedition was ready to press farther into the gloom of the forest. The ground seesawed up one steep ridge and down another. Gabe preferred riding through the fir trees; the huge branches with their profusion of needles cushioned the brunt of the storm. In the open draws, the rain beat down and a sharp wind buffeted him. But at midmorning he looked skyward and saw that the wind was driving the rain clouds eastward. Good! *Tibi tsic djant.* Heap good!

Soon they came to a ridge so steep that all had to dismount and help haul the horses to the top. Such exertion at high altitude was hard on the older men. Several became nauseated, and Washburn suffered a severe nosebleed. From the top, Gabe looked out over mile upon mile of jumbled timberland and glowering peaks. He strained to see the streak of yellow that would pinpoint the canyon, but saw none. No matter. He knew it was thar. *There!*

"Is that where we're going?" Nute asked worriedly. The others were also disgruntled by the forbidding picture. "Mountain, mountains," Jake grumbled. "Where are these natural wonders you bragged up, Langford? Anyone can see there isn't anything beyond here worth going on for. Let's go home."

No, Gabe thought, barely hiding his exasperation, we are *not*, absolutely, positively *not* turning back. That Jake. *Yagaki!* Squaller! Then he chuckled, because having a secret nickname for Jake somehow made him easier to bear. But something exciting had better turn up pretty soon, or else Jake might win support from the men, who were becoming more and more disillusioned. Gabe could hear them muttering that it might be a good idea after all to return to Helena.

Then the Yellowstone and the weather relented. The trail crossed pleasant grassland. The wind tore the clouds to pieces, and bold shafts of light probed the forest and meadows, the golden light reflecting myriads of diamond-bright crystals on the dripping rocks and shrubs. As the sun warmed the men and dried their clothing, their spirits brightened. Gabe whistled a happy, tuneless song as he rode along.

At midday all rested in a clearing beside a small warm spring which bubbled weakly and smelled a little like rot-

62

ten eggs. After pinching his glasses on the bridge of his nose, Everts peered at it and asked, "Is this one of those supposedly horrendous boiling springs we've heard so much about? This one seems rather tame."

Even Gabe was a little shaken. This uninteresting little pool wasn't what he had expected.

"Some puddle!" Jake taunted Langford. "You told us we'd see boiling springs that spouted a hundred feet in the air!"

"We will, we will," Langford answered confidently. "Just give me time."

"How much time?" Jake demanded. "We've been on the road ten days already and haven't seen a durn thing but mountains, and that's nothin' to holler about in Montana. Half of us have colds, we're all stove up from sleeping on the ground, we're—"

"Then why don't you go home?" snapped Hauser.

"When I turn back," Jake grunted, "I'll have enough of you with me so you'll all have to go."

Gabe served the coffee and sat cross-legged on the ground to eat his beans and cold biscuit. How to keep the expedition headed south? The only way was to reach that yellow canyon soon. If only he could slip off and do a little exploring on his own. He paused, the knife halfway to his mouth. Why couldn't he? He wasn't afraid of getting lost, and he could cover a lot more territory than the sluggish pack train. Mr. Langford would be angry, but that wasn't much of a risk. Besides, it was time he limbered up the Winchester and brought in some fresh meat.

Two soldiers stood guard; the others dozed, hats over their faces. Cautiously Gabe led the pinto out of sight. Then he sprang into the saddle, slapped the reins on

63

Tibo's rump, and tore off. Atop the next ridge he drew rein, shaded his eyes with his hand, and looked out across the country. He saw sun and blue sky. What a difference! The Yellowstone was smiling and radiant, but secretive, giving no indication of the whereabouts of the yellow canyon.

He rode on. Once more the air was filled with bird song and smelled less of wet forest duff. Chipmunks scampered or sunned themselves. He whistled at them, and they popped up on their blunt haunches, wrinkling their noses at him. He laughed, no longer feeling alone. He came to a clearing and saw it formed an unobstructed approach to the river, so he rode to the edge.

Ayeeee! He greeted the foaming green torrent with joy. The canyon had deepened several hundred feet, and the buckskin-colored banks were so eroded that they appeared carved into so many tepees. Wait till the men saw this! Following a game trail upriver, he came upon a lone, soaring pillar of gray pitted rock. His heart began to pound. This must be *The Needle*! Jim Bridger had called it that to describe a gaunt column over two hundred and fifty feet high. "Good thing I found it," Bridger had told him. "My leggings was a sorry sight. I set right down thar and pulled the rips together with that thar needle. Then I poked it back in place for the next fellow to use. Mind now, if you use it, put it back."

Once more laughter bubbled from Gabe's lips as he figured how he would keep a straight face when he told Bridger that he had found The Needle. "Best needle in the world," he'd say. "Wish't I could've brung it with me. But I done what you told me. I put it back."

When fallen timber blocked his way, he retraced his

path, blazing the trees along it. On the main trail where the pack train would pass he forked two peeled willow shoots, keeping them upright by laying a longer one in the crotch and pointing it toward the river. The General or Mr. Langford would surely see the sign and follow it.

He rode on, not fast enough to miss anything. The trees closed about him, then thinned again. There, ahead on the trail, their buff hides blending with the sun-cured grass, stood two antelope. *"Kwaditsi!"* he exclaimed, sucking in his breath. He checked Tibo and unholstered the rifle, but need not have hurried. The antelope watched him, not alarmed, sniffing to get his scent. When Gabe and the pinto remained motionless they soon lowered their heads and resumed feeding.

He started to raise his gun, but stopped. There was something strange here. He had the craziest feeling that these antelope, usually so quick to bolt, *accepted* him. He looked around at a woodpecker hammering away at a tree trunk, at squirrels and chipmunks that chirred but didn't *scold*. There was none of the breathless silence that usually enveloped a forest when an enemy appeared.

He couldn't bear to shatter the lovely peace by firing his gun, so he toed the pinto gently and moved along at a natural walk. Unconcernedly the antelope drifted away. Then he rode faster toward the southwest and forded a small creek. Upstream he spotted a beaver dam. Live beaver were a rarity because most mountain streams had been stripped years ago during the merciless slaughter for pelts. He dismounted and crept up the bank.

Bang! The sentry beaver slapped the black water with his paddle-shaped tail, and several others slipped into the water. Gabe giggled nervously; the noise had almost scared him right out of his moccasins! He crouched behind an aspen, waiting until the sentry surfaced, swam about, then dove again and reappeared with young ones who climbed onto the mud-and-stick dam.

After a while Gabe withdrew reluctantly, mounted Tibo, and rode on. Another mile, another beaver dam— and a moose standing hock deep in the pond to feed on underwater plants. It plunged its big head with the ugly horns under the surface and raised it, muzzle dripping, as its black lips sucked the stalks into its mouth. The moose, too, ignored him. Gabe was glad to see a moose; along with elk and deer, they had been driven back, farther and farther, higher and higher, by the advancing settlers and hunters.

He pressed on, thinking how wonderful it was that here was at least one secret place, one haven— He reined in, thinking with mounting excitement. Was this the great truth about the Yellowstone that Bridger had said he must discover for himself? That here was one place where wild game did not flee in terror at the slightest alien sight or sound; where the wilderness existed just as it had for centuries; where the rocks had never echoed the murderous whack of a bullet; where man had not intruded, save perhaps red men who stalked silently with bow and arrow to kill only so as not to starve, and then slipped away without leaving an ugly scar to record their passing?

He clasped his arms over his ribs to contain his joy. The Yellowstone was a natural sanctuary for wild animals! A white man might not sense this, but Bridger had hoped that he, a half-Indian, might. Now he knew, he knew, and just wait until he told— His heartbeat slowed. But he wouldn't, he couldn't, tell this secret—not to men like Mr. Langford and his friends, who hoped to find out whether or not the Upper Yellowstone was suitable for settlement. That would mean an invasion of people, with their wagons and cabins, and cows eating the good grass, and roads, and many hunters. He stiffened. No, sirreeee, he wouldn't tell the Yellowstone's secret. He'd —why, he'd do *anything* to keep the Yellowstone just the way it was.

For one wild moment he wanted to lose himself in the woods, but hard on the thought came the realization that he must return to the expedition. So he retraced his route, and when he came to a grassy draw, his obligation as a hunter forced him to fire on a young deer. Intent only on his target and later on dressing it out, he took little note of his surroundings. Only when he raised his head to wipe the perspiration off his forehead did he see something that brought him bolt upright.

"The jewel tree!" he exclaimed aloud, the jewel tree Bridger had told him about, sparkling with rubies and emeralds and diamonds! The old pathfinder had had to explain what jewels were and how men craved them before Gabe's desire to see the jewel tree had been truly aroused. He ran forward, eager to fill his fists, but as he touched them, he discovered the jewels were only bits of colored stone glittering in the sunshine on a tree trunk that itself was of stone. Disappointment washed out his joy. Worse, he felt silly. But then, as he ran his fingers over the trunk, memory served him, and he laughed in spite of himself.

What a good joke Bridger had pulled on him, or anybody else who searched, hoping to find a real jewel tree. This could only be Old Gabe's famous "peetrified" tree.

That was something he could tell Mr. Langford, and he gathered a handful of petrified chips to show him. Then he hefted the light carcass on the pinto, who shied and tossed his head, but nevertheless carried him back to his friends. Since the riders and pack train had continued up the river trail, it was not long before Gabe located them. Mr. Langford rode swiftly to his side. "Gabe, I swear I don't know whether to hug you or larrup you! We thought you were lost!"

"*Ah hi e!*" Gabe greeted his friend. "I warn't lost, I went exploring. Did you find my blaze pointing toward the river? Did you see how steep the canyon is now? Did you find The Needle?"

Langford said that they had, but there was something about the look on his face that made Gabe forget the petrified chips and ask anxiously, "Didn't you like it?"

"Yes, I liked it," Langford admitted readily, "but Jake and some of the others—" He hesitated, and his fist clenched the saddle horn. "If Washburn gave the word, there are five who would turn back right now. Oh, if only that warm pool we stopped by had been a big spouter, or the canyon deeper and a bright yellow!"

"You wouldn't turn back, would you?"

"No," Langford assured Gabe, "but if the others do that defeats the purpose of this expedition. You see, I organized an expedition instead of a small party of two or three because it's important that a number of men, and particularly prominent citizens, verify the wonders of the Yellowstone. The public would accept an expedition report, but they would just laugh at you and me, the same way they laughed at Bridger."

Gabe thought hard. How could he help Mr. Langford?

He just had to help, and the best way would be to locate the yellow canyon. Could he? Today, maybe? He
struggled to recall all that Bridger had told him about the
approach to it. After you crossed the Gardner and went
a considerable distance through the timber, you came to a
creek, a big one full of rocks and cascades, and followed
it to the canyon. He studied the sky anxiously; yes, there
were several hours of sunlight remaining, not counting the
long afterglow. Then he looked at Mr. Langford and
wanted so badly to say something to cheer him up that
he blurted with more confidence than he actually felt, "I
bet I know where we turn off to the canyon." When Mr.
Langford's face lit up he grew bolder and said, "I bet you
'n' me could find it today if we went exploring on our
own."

Langford shouted to General Washburn, "Gabe says
that if we can make better time he can lead us to the grand
canyon today."

Gabe's jaw sagged. He'd never said that, never, nor
hadn't said *for sure*. What possessed Mr. Langford to blab
it out loud? Oh, golly, now Hauser and Hedges were urg-
ing the General to let them ride in advance, too. He felt
trapped. What if he couldn't find the canyon? What if he
disappointed them? But he wouldn't; not if the Yellowstone didn't let him down. It hadn't so far, he remembered,
with some returning confidence.

Since the trail had improved somewhat, Washburn decided that a few could be spared from the pack train.
When he and Langford, Hedges, Hauser, and Jake were
ready and the wrangler had removed the deer carcass from
Tibo's back and loaded it on one of the pack mules, he
told Gabe, "Lead the way, young man."

Gabe took a deep breath. Here was another test of his faith in the Yellowstone. All right, get on with it! He clucked to Tibo and started off. But as they rode on and on and on without coming to any creek, he grew worried. The sun was in the west now and soon would cast shadows across the trail. A mile farther on he reined up alongside a wide creek, where the water dashed around a pile of gray boulders. Was this the right creek? It must be. For a moment he hesitated. It had better be the right creek!

"Is this where we turn off?" the General asked.

No use saying maybe, or I guess so; he nodded and knew he was committed. Do, or die for shame. Like daring to run the gantlet in Indian games. You could do it if you set your sights *beyond* the last man and raced through with all your heart and strength.

He pursued a game trail that ran along the north bank over uneven ground and through heavy timber. The boulders in the creek grew larger and larger until they soared like stone towers. One looked like a giant-sized broken hoof, and Gabe heard Jake joking about its being the Devil's Hoof. Finally the way became so tangled that Gabe dismounted and proceeded on foot through heavy brush and windfalls, the others trailing behind.

When Gabe spotted a long outcropping of rock ahead and an opening beyond it, he started running. Bridger had mentioned a rocky ledge from which you could see the tremendous falls. He whooped and ran faster. He couldn't wait to stand at the edge of the yellow canyon and feel the spray from the falls cooling his face.

When he stopped abruptly at the brink and looked into

the gorge, he gasped. Then he felt as if he were turning to ice. This was no mile-deep, yawning chasm, nor was there a trace of yellow anywhere! There was only a deep, rocky gorge where a waterfall gushed between two stone towers and splashed a hundred feet to more gray rocks below! Gabe was so shocked that he couldn't face the others, but he could hear them voicing their disappointment. Worse, Jake began to laugh, loud and forced; he hooted and slapped his knees and jeered, "Some grand canyon!"

Jake's laughter stung like a swarm of hornets. Gabe wheeled around, his eyes blazing, and declared, "This ain't the grand canyon. It—it ain't deep enough. It ain't yellow. It—" But he couldn't go on because he was so humiliated at the way the Yellowstone had failed him.

The others glared at Jake, and the Judge said stoutly, "It may not be the grand canyon, but it's beautiful! Gabe, what did Bridger call this? Do you remember?"

Too upset to appreciate the beauty of the rocky glen and waterfall, Gabe hung his head. "He never, *never* told me about a place like this."

Hauser snapped his fingers. "Then you've made a discovery all your own. You're an explorer!"

"Explorer, my foot," Jake said disgustedly. "When are you men going to stop kidding yourselves into believing that old liar Bridger's tales? This is the grand canyon, and that's the falls of the Yellowstone, and now that we've all got saddle sores for our trouble, we can head back to Helena tomorrow." He stomped back to his horse.

Gabe's head snapped up. He looked for Mr. Langford to say, "We most certainly are not turning back!" But he didn't say a word, nor did the others. Gabe's heart sank as he realized they weren't putting up any argument at all.

He turned his back on the falls and shuffled over to Tibo. He couldn't have felt worse if the Yellowstone had slapped him in the face.

V

The Yellow Canyon

THE next morning Gabe wakened long before sunrise. His blankets were stiff with a feathery coating of ice, and it was so cold he was torn between a desire to linger under his covers and an eagerness to join General Washburn, who was building up the campfire. He burrowed deeper under the blankets and shut his eyes, but sleep evaded him, and he knew why. He dreaded getting up because today the expedition was to turn back to Helena.

For a few seconds he wallowed in self-pity. It didn't help matters to know that he and not the Yellowstone was at fault. He'd followed the wrong creek and then had felt betrayed and humiliated when the Yellowstone didn't produce the yellow canyon for him to flaunt before Jake. Now he wouldn't have a second chance. He lay on his back, feeling sorrier and sorrier for himself. Goodbye, Yellowstone!

Then he got so disgusted with himself that he rolled

73

over on his stomach and wrestled with the problem of how to hold back the expedition a day or two. Could he play sick? No, that wouldn't work because he was simply too healthy. What about asking Jake to give him another day? No, he wouldn't lower himself to do that. Well, what else was there? Nothing, just plain nothing.

He pulled up a blade of grass and chewed on it. Come to think of it, he didn't have to go back to Helena. He could— He flipped over and sat bolt upright. Yes, he could slip away and explore the Upper Yellowstone on his own! Anyway, he owed that much to Old Gabe. He just couldn't go back to Bridger's farm and confess, "I didn't see the yellow canyon, or nothin'." Why? Well, uh, he hadn't tried hard enough.

Now look here, he told himself sternly, face the truth; to make Old Gabe happy wasn't the real reason he wanted to go on. He just wasn't going to let the Yellowstone get the best of him without a struggle. He was reminded of the first time he had wrestled an older Shoshone boy and got his nose bloodied and ran bellowing to his father. Pa had made him go back and pitch in, even though he was sure to lose. Well, he'd better tackle the Yellowstone the same way. The Yellowstone wasn't any tougher than the Absaroka to the east, or the Tetons to the south, where he had hunted with his father and the Indians. He could live on game meat and water, like Bridger and his Pa had done many a time, and he could survive, no doubt about it. Ayeeee! How else to find out whether or not he had the makings of a real mountain man.

Then Gabe remembered he'd have to leave Tibo. The pinto didn't belong to him, and he would take only his packsack and rifle. He made a face; too bad, he'd miss Tibo a lot. But the Yellowstone was more important.

He wriggled quietly out of his blankets, rolled them, and slipped them under the flap of the packsack. Then he picked up his rifle and pack and started to tiptoe toward the brush. He hadn't gone two steps in the gray light when he stepped on a dry branch. Cr-ack!

General Washburn glanced over his shoulder. "Oh, it's you, Gabe. Bring the coffeepot, will you?" He spoke softly so as not to waken the others.

Gabe had to count to ten before he could answer, "All right." Of all the stupid—! Couldn't he do *anything* right? He put down the pack and rifle and fetched the leftover coffee and the tin cups.

The General noticed he was upset. "What's the matter, lad?"

"Nothin'," he answered grumpily. While the coffee heated, he stared glumly at the fire. When Washburn said, "You know a lot more about this country than the rest of us, don't you?" Gabe winced and replied, "After what happened yesterday, I ain't so sure I know anything about it."

Washburn chuckled. "Nonsense. You aren't the first explorer who set out to look for one thing and stumbled onto something else."

Explorer? He was an explorer? Gabe rubbed his heels in the dirt. "You're just trying to make me feel better." As soon as steam curled from the spout he filled the cups.

"Aaah," Washburn murmured, gratified. "This is the life. No need to be on parade all the time. No bothering about rank. Beautiful country inspires a man, makes him relax." He rubbed his whiskered cheeks. He'd

75

stopped shaving, his hair wasn't combed, and his clothing was disheveled. Once he had realized he wasn't expected to be the military type of leader, he had begun to enjoy himself.

Gabe, studying him covertly, was thinking that the Yellowstone had surely changed the General. He'd stopped barking orders; instead of having others wait on him, he helped with the tents and cut firewood. And he did double his share of guard duty after he found out Jake, when it was his turn for night patrol, whipped back into his tent after the first quarter hour and left his partner, poor-sighted, elderly Mr. Everts, to stumble around by himself. In Gabe's eyes the General was all right.

"Well, young man," Washburn said suddenly, "do you think we can find the yellow canyon today?"

Gabe's mouth was full of coffee, and he almost choked, stammering, "To—today? Aren't you turning back today?"

Today was Sunday, the General explained, and added knowingly, his eyes twinkling, "I didn't have the least trouble convincing Jake and his friends that since we had been on the road eleven days, we really should have a day of rest before turning back. Of course, I didn't let on that what I really wanted was one more day to find that grand canyon."

Gabe jumped to his feet. "Can I go with you? Can we start right now?"

Washburn thought a moment, then drained his cup. "Yes, let's saddle up."

After they had ridden about a mile from camp Washburn suggested companionably, "What would you think about climbing one of these mountains close by to see if we can locate the canyon?"

Having the leader ask his opinion pleased Gabe, and his cheeks flushed as he replied, "That's a swell idea."

The two followed a twisting game trail through the shadowy forest. Tibo shied at the brush and overhanging branches, mostly for fun, because it was chilly and he was impatient to race, instead of plodding along a lane through trees. The first trail they followed led the men to a swamp. They laughed and scouted around, Tibo trying to crowd the General's mare on the narrow trail, until Gabe held his head back so far that he decided to calm down. Finally the riders got onto another trail that led upward. Before long they were skirting snowbanks, and an hour later had climbed to timberline. After one look at the jumbled rock on the mountainside, both dismounted, picketed their horses, and continued on foot. Burning with eagerness, Gabe forged ahead.

Suddenly he was on the summit. "Ayeee! There it is!" He ripped off his headband and waved it wildly. As Washburn joined him, he pointed across a vast stretch of sky to the wide mouth of an undeniably yellow canyon. Immense clouds of spray billowed above a tremendous waterfall. Beyond it was a green valley and farther off, a long, long stretch of blue water. The Teton's stony purple flanks and snow-capped peaks soared on the horizon. "*Tibi tsic djant*," he shouted over and over. Heap good; very heap good!

Washburn let out three short-breathed cheers.

The Upper Yellowstone was a high plateau walled in on all sides by mountains. No wonder it was hard to reach the heart of it; during all but the few summer months deep snow would hold back intruders, and the difficult trail would discourage all but the most determined. He grinned; it hadn't stopped Washburn or Langford, or Gabe himself.

As he and the General faced eastward, the sky began to blossom with delicate patches of pink and yellow. As the sun rose above the Absaroka, these deepened in color, the lemon-clear light bathing granite ridges, flooding down across timbered slopes, and driving the mist from dark gullies. The entire amphitheater radiated with a fresh, brilliant beauty.

"We've got to bring the others up here," Washburn declared. He put an arm on Gabe's shoulder and gave him an affectionate hug. "Won't Langford be surprised?"

Gabe was shivering with joy, scarcely able to contain his elation. "Won't Jake be surprised?" he gloated. "When the others see this, they won't turn back."

A few moments later they picked their way down the mountainside and then rode pell-mell to camp. Gabe gave Tibo his head and let him run out all his devilment. As they rushed in, the men dropped their plates and jumped to their feet. Washburn flung himself out of the saddle, shouting, "We've seen the canyon and falls and the lake from a mountain top nearby. Come on! Gabe and I will show you!"

Within seconds the campsite was deserted. Hearts strained in the race to the summit. When Langford saw the canyon and lake he was so overwhelmed that all he could say was, "My prayers have been answered."

"Let's not dally here," Hauser urged, after noting the direction with his compass. "Let's get on to the canyon."

Although the others were enthusiastic about the idea, Gabe glanced apprehensively at Jake, for fear the argumentative fellow would refuse. When he made no objection Gabe felt as if a ton of worry had fallen from his shoulders; he felt a foot taller and bursting with happiness. He would have liked to remain on top of the mountain all day, but the desire to reach the canyon was even stronger. Too bad he couldn't flap his arms and fly straight to it like a crow!

However, glimpsing the canyon from a mountain, which the men named Mount Washburn in honor of their leader, and getting to it by ground travel were two very different matters. After two unsuccessful days and nights, Gabe wasn't sure who was battling the hardest, the men who were struggling through the dense forest and over an exasperatingly difficult trail or the Yellowstone itself, which seemed set on preventing their reaching the golden prize.

The expedition pushed on at daybreak, without breakfast, and finally, shortly before sunrise on Wednesday, August thirty-first, Gabe hurrahed as he caught sight of the radiant glow of the chasm reflecting through the trees. Dismounting hurriedly and picketing Tibo, he ran ahead to look for the jutting rock which Bridger had assured him was there. He found it easily and soon was peering eagerly over the edge. Ayeeee! the whole world seemed to slide down in a dizzying plunge of yellow rock. He swayed and dropped to his knees, clutching the edge with his fingers, blinking and squinting in the blinding light. Then he cocked his head to one side, listening intently to a deep-throated thundering. But it couldn't be thunder! He glanced upward and saw the falls. "O-h,"

79

he murmured, exhaling slowly. Although the gigantic cataract was a half mile upstream, the fall of water was so tremendous that the rumble of its thunder rolled over him. He stretched out as far as he dared, to see the river, a thousand feet below, looking like a rumpled green banner whipping in the wind. When Langford and Washburn knelt beside him, he pointed out the falls.

"Jehoshaphat! It's twice as high as Niagara!" Washburn had to shout to be heard.

Gabe felt someone leaning on his shoulders; it was Jake, pressing forward to view the canyon. "Some hole, ain't it?" he wisecracked. "Almost as big as the one in my stomach." After a brief glance, he turned away, yelling for Nute to get on with breakfast.

Distressed at the thought of having to tear himself away from the canyon and help with the cooking, Gabe appealed to Washburn, "Do I have to go now?"

The General turned to Langford. "How about letting Gabe have the whole day to himself?"

When Langford nodded Gabe blurted, "Golly, thanks!" Once more he faced the canyon. The sun was rising above the trees on the opposite bank, wave upon wave of pastel pink and yellow light momentarily tinting the white cataract. As the sunlight brightened Gabe vowed he could hear the colors crackling. For a moment he thought his heart would burst right out of his chest. The deep, steep gorge blazed with many colors, but mostly with the bold, vibrant yellow that was as vivid as a goldfinch's feathers. The sloping, nearly vertical walls were deeply eroded and carved into many pinnacles tipped and streaked with colors ranging from ivory to deep orange, blood-red, and brown. The dark evergreens provided a striking contrast, not only along the rim, but far below, wherever pines had taken root on inaccessible ledges.

In the mist rising from the falls rainbows arched and faded. When Gabe saw where wild game had scratched hairline trails down to the river he shouted, "I'm going down there!" Before Langford could caution, "Now be careful," he was running light-footed back to the rim, then along its edge until he found just such a trail. He started down, bent-kneed at first, later crawling and sliding until he was at the bottom of the gorge. He was dripping with perspiration from the exertion and the sun's heat reflecting from the steep walls.

Once more he longed to roll and wallow in the Yellowstone, so off came the buckskins and moccasins, and he waded in. Although the water was only knee deep, the current almost bowled him over. He squatted down and let it beat over him, then leaned back and let it run through his hair. The rim seemed far, far away, and Langford and Hauser, working their way down, looked like beetles inching over the yellow rock. By the time they reached the river, he was ready to follow them to the foot of the falls. The blast of wind and spray stirred up by the falls almost knocked him down, and the roaring was so terrible that he plugged his ears with his fingers.

When the men beckoned, he accompanied them on the long, arduous climb to the top. They had to stop every few minutes to "blow" and had to lie down on the grass and get their wind when they reached the rim, but he left them and ranged far along the edge. "*Ah hi e*," he greeted the canyon over and over and laughed because he was sure the canyon shouted back, "Yellow, yellow! *Mi tsi a di zi!*" It was yellow, all right.

Suddenly he had to know what was above the falls, so he retraced his path and passed Langford and Hauser, who were measuring the depth of the falls by doling out lengths of weighted rope. He pushed on upriver. Before long, he discovered that the Yellowstone burst through narrow rocky jaws in a second waterfall, only about one-third as large as the lower fall. Gabe slid down a muddy trail to its base, stripped again, and waded out to a point where the sidelash beat on him. He closed his eyes and held his nose, reveling in the icy water splashing over his head and face. When he had had enough he climbed to the rim and continued on upriver along the shaded banks until the trees thinned out and he looked out across miles of rolling meadowland. This was the valley he had seen from atop Mount Washburn; he would be sure to tell the General that it was easy going to the lake, just in case Jake got the notion to turn back now that the expedition had reached the Grand Canyon of the Yellowstone.

A sweet scent sent him scurrying around the edge of the woods until he found a patch of huckleberries and wild strawberries. He rooted through them like a bear and ate until he was full and his hands and mouth were sticky. No matter. He washed in the river, then meandered back toward camp. Along the way he whistled at kingfishers and chipmunks, watched trout dart away when his shadow darkened the water, and plucked a fringed purple gentian for his headband. Shadows overlay the entire canyon when he returned to the campsite, and the wind had stilled. The pulsating drumming of the falls could be heard even above the cheerful crackling of the fire.

"Have a good day?" the General and Judge asked as Gabe made the rounds of the skillets. He nodded happily and loaded his plate with antelope steak, roast duck, fried potatoes, biscuits and gravy, and when he was almost, but not quite, as full as a tick, he tried some of Nute's wild gooseberry cobbler. Then, wiping his face on his sleeve, he told the cook, "I should have come back in time to help you with supper. I'll do all the chores tonight."

After these were done, he stretched full length by the campfire, his head propped on his arms. Although the men talked and talked about the canyon and falls, he didn't join in the conversation. Somehow he figured that if he opened his mouth, his happiness would dribble out, and he wanted to hoard every bit of joy inside himself.

Besides, he didn't even want to listen to human talk. He hearkened instead to the song of the Yellowstone. The hair on the back of his neck prickled as he heard the mellow night song of the horned owl rolling through the pines, the high squeaking of the flying squirrels that swerved over his head through firelight and shadow, and from far off the yap-yap-yipeeee of a coyote. The tree trunks creaked softly, the wind soughed through the evergreens, the falls drummed their ancient rhythm—low-keyed, ageless, like the Shoshone drums communing with the Great Spirit.

When had he ever been more content? Never. He was at peace with himself, with the Yellowstone, with Bridger, and with his friends, who could scarcely wait for morning to push on to the lake.

PENINSULAR

VI

Battle with a Dragon

THE next morning was the kind that tripped Gabe into thinking that he had licked the Yellowstone with one hand behind his back.

This first day of September heralded the approach of Indian summer with a deep blue, cloudless sky, hot sunlight, and grass-scented breeze. The riders soon strung out at a good pace across a gently rolling valley. Not knowing exactly how far it was to the lake, General Washburn had asked all the men to escort the pack train, so there would be no hunting until later in the afternoon. As Gabe rode midway along the line of mules, he saw yellow in the knee-high grass, in the bright faces of paintbrush and daisies, on frost-nipped aspen leaves on the few trees providing islands of shade near the river. No wonder yellow was the "sign" of the Yellowstone, he thought—a kind of Indian owner stick, painted and adorned to represent the owner's name.

84

He couldn't wait to see the lake, and after that—well, what after that? He frowned and squirmed a little. Gosh, after that the expedition would be almost over, without the Yellowstone's having provided even half the excitement he had anticipated. Oh, he would have seen the canyon and falls and the lake, just about everything Bridger had talked sensible about except those spouters. But since discovering the jewel tree, Gabe wasn't sure that the spouters weren't more of the old pathfinder's jokes. After all, how would a pool spout? Straight up, hard, and explosive like a mountain man's belch, or sidewise like a trapper spitting tobacco juice? He laughed out loud.

The farther he rode the more he succumbed to needle-sharp pricks of dissatisfaction. He hadn't found the answer to the rest of Bridger's stories; there was no glass mountain, no pool with a fire in the bottom, no river that ran both hot and cold. It was too bad to have to admit they were jokes.

But Mr. Langford was content. "I don't care if we never see another blessed thing. To me the canyon was the thrill of a lifetime."

Judge Hedges remarked, "Well, I won't be satisfied until I've fished in that lake."

Gabe felt guilty for not being more satisfied; nor could he decide in what way the Yellowstone could provide more of the personal challenge he had wanted. Not that he wanted to invite danger, but so far he hadn't encountered any real danger, only some worry, and the one big disappointment that had happily turned out to be Tower Falls. There was Jake, of course, and now that Gabe's concern over the canyon was over and Jake was no longer a threat to their progress, what could he expect in the way

85

of an honest-to-goodness contest? Not much; after all, the Yellowstone wasn't so tough!

At midmorning, when the expedition came to a creek about two feet wide and two inches deep, General Washburn signalled a stop. Gabe dismounted and led the pinto to water. Tibo lowered his head and sucked greedily, then snorted and backed away. "Hieeee-yuh, what's the matter?" Gabe exclaimed, quieting him. Curious, he knelt to drink from cupped hands. After one swallow, he spat it out. "Agh, it's sour!" He noticed the other horses behaving badly and heard Hauser shout, "Don't drink! The water is full of alum."

Alum? Alum? There was something familiar about the word. Gabe wet a finger and licked it. His lips felt as if drawn tight with a sinew thread; his mouth puckered. Suddenly he remembered and jumped to his feet, shouting to Mr. Langford, "This must be Old Gabe's Alum Creek. Remember?"

Mr. Langford had spat the bitter water on the ground. "You're right! Yes, I remember."

"Remember what?" Hauser asked, cursing and wiping his mouth on his shirt sleeve.

"Bridger's story about a creek so full of alum that when he sprinkled some on the trail," said Langford, "it puckered the distance so much he ended up only a few steps from the lake."

While the men chuckled, Gabe remembered something else. He shucked his moccasins and waded into the creek; after soaking his feet for a minute he lifted first one foot, then the other, and finally muttered, "Aw, it don't either."

"Don't what?" Judge Hedges asked.

Gabe grinned sheepishly. "Bridger told me that when

86

elk waded through Alum Creek their hooves shrunk till they were no bigger than a pronghorn kid's. But I don't see my feet shrinking none."

Jake scoffed, "Too bad Bridger didn't dunk his head in Alum Creek. Might've shrunk his tongue so he couldn't tell such whopping lies."

Gabe wished somebody would push Jake in the creek and pucker *his* mouth, but didn't say so aloud. At the canyon he had decided not to let Jake spoil the Yellowstone for him. He could swagger around in his frock coat and bang away half the day, and Gabe would ignore him, though it was hard not to laugh at Jake's hat so full of holes and that awful celluloid collar.

"Let's get on," Washburn rallied the men. "We'll water the stock at the next creek."

Gabe jumped out, dried his feet on the grass, slipped on his moccasins, and mounted Tibo. As he rode along he saw many tracks of wild game, even some of buffalo. Now that was something! He hadn't thought there were any buffalo in this high country. He would look sharply and maybe provide a real treat for dinner. A hunter wasn't a real hunter until he brought down buffalo and had eaten his fill of the braised ribs and tender hump. Right now there wasn't an animal in sight, and no wonder; beads of perspiration were trickling down his neck, and he had to turn over the sweatband to the dry side.

Occasionally in the next hour, when the breeze swirled from the southwest, he wrinkled his nose at an offensive odor. Was there a carcass putrefying nearby? No, perhaps not. A tiny finger of fear poked at him; he stiffened and shrunk a little inside his buckskin shirt. Surely they weren't nearing that dreaded abode of the evil spirits?

But then he got another, stronger whiff. Why, it was like the unpleasant smell of that warm spring where they had lunched days ago. Mr. Langford had called it a "rotten egg" smell. Excitement banished his momentary uneasiness. Maybe they were coming to another warm spring, a bigger one—maybe a spouter!

Farther along the grass thinned out abruptly, and the expedition halted at the edge of a parched, treeless basin. Washburn pointed excitedly. "Look at those boiling springs! I'll bet there're at least fifty!"

"By Jove, a real thermal area!" declared Langford in his ponderous way.

Gabe tensed, his nostrils stung by the strong breath of the sulphur. Above the pools, streamers of steam writhed in the fitful breeze and clouded the sun, so that shadows flickered across the basin. These scared Tibo; he danced sideways and tossed his head, but Gabe talked and patted and was firm on the rein until the little horse quieted.

Coming up behind, Stickney shouted, "Let's have a closer look!" and spurred his horse out onto the whitened crust. A few followed, but quickly checkreined when their horses' hoofbeats gave off an alarming echo. A cloud of steam swirled over Stickney; his horse reared, neighing shrilly, then bucked in terror. Its front feet broke through the crust; steam and scalding mud hissed through the opening and sprayed its legs and belly. The horse screamed, pitched Stickney to the ground, and bolted across the basin, suffering countless more burns as the brittle surface cracked repeatedly under its frenzied plunges.

Swiftly Langford dismounted, tossed his reins to Hauser, and ran to Stickney's aid. As soon as Hauser saw that

Stickney was not injured, he raced around the outer edge of the basin, caught up with the doomed horse, and put it out of its misery.

In spite of the accident, Langford and the others, even Stickney and the usually timid Nute, were anxious to examine the many odd-sized springs and decided they could do so safely if they spread out over the basin and were careful. After picketing their horses on the grass, they set out in twos and threes.

Judge Hedges tarried while Gabe calmed Tibo and set the picket pin firmly in the tough sod. "Want to keep me company?" he invited Gabe.

"You—you go on," Gabe answered. He was wary and wanted more time. His friends might walk boldly onto the crust, but not he. He could only venture out as an Indian would, on guard, sniffing out danger, placing his moccasined steps with infinite care. Although his friends strode to the crusted edges of the boiling springs and peered into their depths, he could not; not he, son of a mountain man and Shoshone mother; not he who had grown tall listening to Old Man tales told before a muttering fire, while the winter wind keened through the tepee smokehole.

No, he was not afraid, he assured himself, only jumpy— and a little confused because he didn't know whether to act as a white man or an Indian. By now he had convinced himself this basin was no abode of evil spirits. After all, he saw with mounting confidence, no poisoning fog hung roundabout, no flames barred the approach to each pool, he heard no fearful growling, as he would if this were that other dreaded place. A little leery of the heat that beat up through his moccasins, he advanced slowly onto

89

the burnt crust, squinting against the glare, knees relaxed, yet ready to spring from danger. He approached the nearest springs; ugh, what foul breath they had! But how beautifully they reflected blue sky. As a cloud of steam enveloped him, he stiffened and stood rigid, scarcely daring to breathe, until it swept away. To quiet his thumping heart he made himself count the ground vents through which the steam curled and puffed. There were too many; don't try. Ayeeee! Suppose the whole crust caved in! But as he looked about he saw no cracks yawning to swallow the others, no part of the ground bending or sinking under their weight. Look with the eyes of a white man, he told himself; don't let those Indian tales make you run for the timber. But it was not easy. . . .

He swallowed the tight anxious knot in his throat and continued on to a placid spring some twenty feet in diameter. One moment the surface was mirror smooth; the next, it started to boil furiously. Bubbles shot up from below, and then from the center an arrow shaft of water soared several feet in the air! He cupped his hands over his mouth. Weaponless, he stood his ground, and for a moment forgetting the "eyes of the white man" he prayed, "*Tomah-upah, tomah-vond, undiddahaidt soondahie!*" Our Father who is above, have mercy!

The Great Spirit protected him, and he was not harmed, and slowly he lowered his hands. Ho! Surely a friendly spirit now spoke to him. The water spout subsided with a merry splash, the surface once more mirror smooth; the pool smiled at him. "*Ah hi e!*" Then he heard someone shout and saw Mr. Langford eagerly waving and pointing to the spring. "Some spouter, eh?"

Spouter! Of course, this was what Bridger meant by a

spouter. No matter that it didn't spout "higher'n a flag-pole," as Bridger had claimed. It was high enough to suit him. Laughing, he answered Langford, "Some spouter! I like!"

He was thankful he had come upon the springs in the company of white men and not with Indians. They had infected him with their courage and lightened his heart with their excitement. There was no telling how he might have acted if he had been out hunting and discovered the hot springs basin all by himself.

He walked lightly to Judge Hedge's side and with him moved farther into the heart of the basin. He stuck his finger in one pool, pulled it out quickly, and blew on it. The water *was* boiling! He heard Nute saying nearby, "I could boil us some meat here 'thout no trouble at all!" Judge Hedges agreed and said it wouldn't be a bad idea to stop and do their laundry as long as there was so much hot water handy.

Gabe looked over his shoulder to see if that water spirit was "talking" again. Sure enough, it spouted again and again. When he stopped beside a large mud pot that was blowing bubbles and suddenly hurled gobs of mud in the air, he wasn't actually afraid, though his stomach turned over with a thump.

Here, too, there was yellow everywhere: in the stunted mustard flowers blooming around the edge of the basin, in the metallic yellow of sunlight reflected in the crystal-clear boiling water, in the yellow and orange tube-throats of the deeper pools, and in the algae coating the channels connecting them. But mostly one noticed it in the brilliant yellow beads of sulphur adorning the edges of some of the hot springs.

"Let me borrow your knife a moment," the Judge asked, and when Gabe handed it to him, Hedges knelt and gently pried loose several of the beads. "Can't go home without some specimens for my boys," he explained as he returned the knife and a bead. Gabe rolled the twinkling, rough little ball in his palm, and joy shot through him. This was a magic piece, an amulet from the heart of the Yellowstone, something to protect him from many dangers. Quickly he tucked it in the secret pocket of the knife sheath. *Tibi tsic djant!*

He was sorry when the General signalled they must leave. Time and time again as they rode southward he breathed deeply to catch the first scent of the lake, but there was only the breath of the sulphur springs. A little farther on he began hearing a strange rumbling, like low-pitched thunder, punctuated now and then by a dull booming. He looked to the sky, but saw no storm clouds. When the noise grew louder, he turned Tibo away from the pack train and rode out fifty yards where he could hear better. When he was sure the sounds were not those of Indian drums, he grew markedly uneasy. Louder. Louder. Now his friends were calling attention to the noise, and the mules were becoming restive. Tibo was balky and fought the jaw rein. Gabe began to worry. Where did that booming come from? He recalled Old Man tales about evil spirits, imprisoned underground, hammering on the earth's crust in their struggle to escape until it heaved and cracked open and hurled helpless victims into its hungry maw. What if some of the evil spirits had already escaped?

An icy blade of fear cut through him from head to toe. Then an explosion rent the air, stampeding the horses and mules. Tibo bolted, but Gabe fought the quivering pinto to a stand. Tense moments passed before the others brought the pack train under control and Gabe had summoned up nerve enough to ask the Judge, "W-what was that awful noise?"

"Sounded like a volcano," Hedges answered, completely bewildering Gabe because he was laughing. Then he sniffed excitedly and added, "Sure smells like one, too."

Volcano? What was a volcano? All Gabe knew was that the rotten egg smell was so strong that he was almost afraid to breathe. He was so confused he didn't know what to think. Hedges and the others, he noticed, weren't the least upset. Was that because the air was poisoning them and making them lunatic?

"Hold the pack train here while we ride forward to investigate the source of that explosion," General Washburn called to the wranglers and soldiers.

Ride forward! Surely that awful noise was caused by the evil spirits or some monster crouching ahead, waiting to gulp down the entire expedition. He tried to warn his friends but couldn't make himself heard. His fear was a live thing now, sucking the strength from his muscles. But if the others rode into danger, he would not desert them; no matter how nervous he was inside he would not show it.

A few moments later he heard a frightful hissing, followed by gurgling and *swallowing* noises! He checked Tibo as the others stopped, thinking they meant to retreat. But no! They scrambled out of their saddles, picketed their mounts hurriedly, and ran forward on foot. Gabe prayed for protection. Such foolishness, to run toward danger, to leave the horses that could whisk them from the clammy fingers of death! Yet he would not hang back; he gritted his teeth and caught up with his friends, though his nostrils were quivering, his throat burned, and his feet were as heavy as grindstones.

He ran past several small hot springs and steam vents and mudholes whose dried sockets seemed to gape malevolently at him. Then he dug in his heels and stopped abruptly before a pulsating pool of boiling water; it poured from a dark cleft mouth at the base of a sage-scabbed foothill—no doubt, the mouth of a monster. It growled, licked its wet chops, and spat several times before lashing out at him with a long scalding tongue of steam and fire. Gabe ducked, dropped flat on his stomach, and dug his fingers into the burnt ground, in case the monster reached out with a wet claw to drag him into its mouth. But he escaped. He heard the monster gulp its rage and hiss repeatedly, though the threats grew weaker. Ayeeee, it was angry because it hadn't captured him! It was recoiling, like a rattlesnake, getting ready to strike again!

But the next sound he heard was *laughter*—Jake's raspy, infuriating guffaw. Startled, afraid his ears were betraying him into a false move, he glanced up. All his friends were ringed behind him, grinning.

After one look at Gabe's face, the fatherly Judge stopped Jake's hooting and strode swiftly to his side. "Gabe, there's nothing to be afraid of. Did you think that was a dragon hissing at you? Those noises are caused by water fluctuating in a tube at the back of that cave." Because he could feel the lad trembling, the Judge added as convincingly as he could, "Believe me, son, this is not the

94

abode of evil spirits, the one you told us about. There is no such place. There are no evil spirits anywhere."

What was he to believe? Gabe flinched as fangs of steam shot out again from the "dragon's mouth." But he was not hurt, and this, along with the Judge's calm, reassuring words, helped quiet his fears. "There aren't any evil spirits? No—no what'd you call it?—no *dragon*?"

No dragon, no monster, no evil spirits; only a fantastic boiling mud spring. The others were all make-believe, the Judge assured him, and real only if you had eyes dimmed with fear and the remembrance of Old Man tales —never real when you looked them square in the face with eyes of courage and intelligence.

Gabe tried hard to understand. Hedges stayed at his side until he was able to watch the "dragon's" antics with increasing pleasure.

Then another loud explosion startled him. The men hurrahed and ran in the direction of the noise. Once more Gabe warred with himself, not knowing whether to run from or toward the unknown.

Judge Hedges suggested, "Let's you and I take it slow. You want to see what is making that noise, don't you?"

Gabe nodded jerkily. What next? What more had the Yellowstone in store for him?

Soon he found himself peering over the rim of a sunken crater; it was partially filled with molten mud. Huge bubbles rose on the surface and broke with the sound of scattering gunfire; the mud drained noisily back into a tube, as if sucked downward by some strange force, then rose rapidly and expelled a foot-thick column of gas and mud to a height of twelve feet.

95

"So that's what makes the explosion!" Hauser exclaimed.

"What makes it?" Gabe asked.

It seemed that because of the depth of the crater, which concentrated the sound of the exploding jet of mud, and the encircling foothills behind the crater, the noise ricocheted like thunder.

While the others were oh-ing and ah-ing, Jake declared in his usual brash manner, "That Dragon's Mouth and this Mud Volcano are worth a hunnert yellow canyons, if you ask me. They're sure different, by golly."

They certainly were, Gabe decided fervently. He'd been frightened before—by rattlesnakes striking unawares, by lightning shattering the cottonwood that sheltered him, by Crows night raiding a Shoshone meat camp, but never, *never* like this. In trying to escape from the Dragon's Mouth it's a wonder he hadn't run blindly into a boiling spring. As he thought about it, he wondered if this was what Bridger had in mind when he had forbidden Gabe to venture alone up the Yellowstone. Did that wise old pathfinder know, as Gabe now knew, that his Indian blood and upbringing might betray him, that for his own good he must be made to meet the Yellowstone on a white man's terms?

He mopped his face. So he had wanted a real testing, had he? Well, he'd had one. Never again would he say the Yellowstone wasn't tough enough to suit him. No, sirreeee!

Slowly happiness chased away the last of his timidity. He'd faced a bigger dragon than any of his young Indian companions; he'd come through his baptism of fear, and his white man's heritage had helped him through.

VII

Buffalo Is the Real
Tobacco Chew!

GABE was drawn out of his thoughts by hearing
General Washburn ask those gathered around the Mud
Volcano, "Shall we scout around some more or return to
our horses?" The General checked his turnip-sized gold
watch, now badly tarnished. "It's past eleven. We should
push on to the lake."

"I'll go fetch the horses," Gabe quickly volunteered—
not just because it was his chore, but because he wanted
the chance to face the Dragon's Mouth alone.

"Shall I go with you?" Judge Hedges offered.

"No, sir." Gabe straightened his shoulders.

"The dragon'll get you if you don't watch out," jeered
Jake.

Gabe eyed Jake coldly. He wanted to say, "The
Crows'll get us if you don't stop shirking your guard

duty." But he held his tongue from such a spiteful outburst; the first part wasn't true; there was little danger now of a Crow attack. Deliberately he turned his back on Jake and walked away. No use letting a mosquito think it had the sting of a deerfly.

He faced the Dragon's Mouth alone, tuned his ear to the gurgling, and dared ask, as a Shoshone would address a powerful water spirit, "*Ah hi e*, mighty spirit, am I not a brave one now?"

The dragon held its tongue for a moment, then hissed, "Ye-s-s-s-s!"

Gabe whooped for joy and ran lightheartedly to the horses. Tibo greeted him with a welcoming neigh and nuzzled him as Gabe pulled the picket pin. He would not gather the others until he had made contact with the pack train.

When Gabe had caught up with them, Elwyn Bean greeted him, "Thought you'd got lost down a hole somewheres."

"I purty near did!" Gabe laughed and described the Dragon's Mouth and Mud Volcano. The wrangler shifted his tobacco cud from one cheek to the other and said he would "go round those mud pots. If the mules see that there volcano blowin' mud at 'em, no rope will hold 'em, and we'll be pickin' our groceries and tents out of every tree between here and the lake." He squinted at Lieutenant Doane. "You agreeable?"

The blond lieutenant nodded and ordered his company of five perspiring privates to mount.

Nute asked, "Gabe, you going to get us some meat for supper?"

"Sure he will!" Bean said, winking at Gabe. "Plenty o'

98

buffler sign along here. Might take some doin', but I been thinkin' it'd be nice if a stripling like you, Gabe, brought in some fat hump and ribs. By hisself, I mean, so we wouldn't have no *crow* served up with the gravy."

So Bean didn't want Jake to get a buffalo, Gabe realized; he wants me to, because I won't sour the meat bragging over it. He smacked his lips and rubbed his stomach. "Buffalo is the real tobacco chew. Like you said, it'll take some doin'. But if I were to set my mind on it— You got something handy I could carry it in?"

The wrangler chuckled and rummaged through one of the packs. "Here's the biggest dang meat sack in the whole outfit." And as Gabe rode off he called, "Luck!"

Gabe led the saddle horses well around the gully where the Dragon's Mouth smoked and soon discovered the men had moved from the Mud Volcano to a new discovery. He held the horses at a safe distance until Washburn and Langford took over; they told him to go see this newest wonder. He hurried through the sagebrush, holding his nose because of the overpowering stench, and joined Judge Hedges. "Phew! what is that?"

"A real mud geyser," the Judge explained. "Since we got here it's been erupting every four minutes. We've been timing it. Watch! See, it tosses gobs of mud twenty feet in the air!"

Gabe eyed the wrinkled, gray, gaping cavity; it reminded him of the mouth of some dreadful monster. Ugh! Its breath made him dizzy. What if he fell into the molten jaws and was sucked down, down, down—! He found himself teetering over the edge and jerked back. Quick! Better think like a white man! "*You* can watch it, but *I'm* going to the river."

99

General Washburn had moved the horses to water, but warned Gabe, "Don't let that pinto drink too much. The water tastes as if some one had emptied a sack of salt in it."

The surface water was roiled by streams of bubbles discharged from subterranean gas vents; these and the run-off from nearby mineral springs made the water unpalatable. Though he was hot and very thirsty, Gabe only rinsed his mouth and then wished he hadn't, because he was left with a foul taste, and his tongue felt furry. He had no trouble restraining Tibo; after one swallow, the little horse snorted and backed away.

Wiping his face with his sleeve, Gabe remarked, "I sure hope it ain't far to the lake. I dunno who's sweating the most, Tibo or me." His buckskin shirt itched and was plastered to his back and shoulders. He wrinkled his nose at his own stale smell; a bath in the lake and a good scrub-down with soapweed was what he needed most.

At that moment Jake, Gillette, Stickney, and Trumbull claimed their horses and announced they were going to ride ahead so they could hunt. General Washburn was agreeable; from what he had seen atop the mountain, the way to the lake was fairly direct. After the four had ridden off at a pace much too fast for horses who had had insufficient water on a hot day, Langford asked Gabe, "Aren't you going hunting with them?"

"Not with Jake," he blurted.

"Don't blame you," Hauser spoke out. "Dang fool gives me the willies, the way he's always shooting past somebody's ear, or riding with his rifle pointed at someone's back."

Already the sound of their gunfire could be heard, and

Gabe had a hunch that every animal this side of the river was running for cover. Good! If the General and Mr. Langford would allow it, he would hunt alone, across the river where he was sure to find a creek that flowed from the mountains on the east. Bridger had told him about it, the one place near the lake where elk and buffalo summered until the first snowfall drove them eastward over a pass to lower country.

"You want to go hunting alone?" Langford objected with that but-you-might-get-hurt look on his face.

"Yes, sir."

"What if you come upon another hot springs basin?"

"I won't be afraid. I won't get lost neither, not this near the lake."

Washburn grunted. "Maybe you'd better hunt across the river if we're to have meat tonight."

"All right," Langford agreed finally, "if you promise to make the lakeshore before dark so you can find our camp."

"Shucks, I'll be back with meat for supper." Gabe spoke confidently, his foot scarcely touching the stirrup as he swung into the saddle. The men stood by until Tibo had picked his way across the river, and Gabe waved before disappearing into the trees.

When the forest thinned out, he turned the pinto southward across open grass. The moment the little beast scented fresh water he laid his ears back and broke into a run, but Gabe hauled in on the reins and held him to a steady trot. He breathed deeply to rid his lungs of the tainted air of the mud springs; it was good to smell evergreen and wild hay and sweet water again. Before long he saw the thick trace of willows bordering the creek—

Pelican Creek, Bridger had called it, because he had once shot one of the lumbering pouch-jawed birds there. Gabe knew what a pelican looked like because the Shoshone medicine man had one mounted in his lodge.

Ayeeee, but he was in a fine mood. Was it only this morning that he had felt let down? That bit of conceit had cost him a hard lesson, but did he care? "No!" he shouted. He laughed aloud and dug in his knees as Tibo shied violently.

The Yellowstone was a great teacher. He was learning many things in the wilderness school: how to live in harmony with the Yellowstone itself, no small feat; how to get along with white men so different from the trappers and frontiersmen he had met at Bridger's fort; how to think more like white men and even tolerate their way of camping. At first he had been secretly scornful of all the foofaraw and the stress on comfort and cleanliness; but once he had grown accustomed to the sight of men doing squaw's work he liked the orderliness and particularly the food—the buttered, salted oatmeal, and soda biscuits, and flapjacks with sweetening, all new to him and putting tallow on his bony frame.

The more he worked with Mr. Bean, the more he thought maybe someday he might be a wrangler. He loathed any place cluttered with dirt and man noises: towns, trading posts, Indian villages, places where you couldn't smell or even hear the outdoors. But the day of the mountain man was over. Come to think of it, he didn't want to be the old-style mountain man like his Pa; he wasn't a lone wolf by nature; he liked *some* company. Best of all he liked the Yellowstone; better than the Absarokas or the Tetons and a lot more than that side-winding dirty snake of a Missouri River! Right now he couldn't think of a better future than earning his way as a wrangler on the Yellowstone. Just thinking about it made him feel steady deep down inside, no longer jumpy wondering where and how a man who was part white and part Indian could make a good life for himself. Not a good *living*, mind you; he wanted to keep his packsack light and his cartridge belt filled and enough food to maintain his strength; a good *life* was his ambition.

This goal needn't be the kind the medicine man pictured after he had smoked peyote and seen a vision of the life ahead of the Shoshones once they had stepped out of their earth bodies. It could be real. Mr. Bean had told him many people would be burning to see the yellow canyon and falls "after Mr. Langford and the General gits through layin' it on. That writing Langford does every night, that's for printin' in newspapers. He's bound and determined that every one in the whole dang country is goin' to know the truth about this here Yellowstone."

Gabe hoped Mr. Bean was right, but whether he was or not, he knew that come spring, he'd hanker to return in the month-of-the-wild-rose blooming, after the high water had receded and snow no longer plugged the mountain trails. He tried to wet his lips, but couldn't. This thirst was nothing compared to the stronger one inside him; he'd developed such a thirst for the Yellowstone that he would be drawn back until every peak, valley, plateau, creek, and "hot" basin were as familiar to him as the lines on the palm of his hand.

They reached the creek and soon he and Tibo were drinking the clear, cold water—just a little at first, to avoid cramps; then Gabe stripped off his buckskins and knelt to scrub himself by wetting and wringing out the head rag. He splashed water on Tibo's head and wiped the little horse's neck and ears with a handful of grass; then he drank again. Pelican Creek here was at least forty paces wide, very shallow, but splashing importantly as big creeks did. After a few moments the finches and blue-birds and blue jays accepted him and the pinto; only the killdeers and spotted sandpipers ran back and forth on the gravelly shore crying nervously until he skittered a stone over the water at them, and they flew away.

He murmured softly to Tibo, "Now our mouths are smooth, we look for *kotea*, the buffalo, eh, little friend?"

Tibo shook his head and turned prankishly so Gabe had to hop like a crow before he could get into the saddle. They moved upstream several miles. Often Gabe's fingers itched for the rifle as he saw elk and antelope grazing on the south slopes of unusually high hills. Once again he marveled at the way the wild ones ignored him, or if the wind off the lake brought them his strange scent, how they drifted off, and *blink!* They vanished into the timber. They were wary because they had known the infrequent thunder of hunters' guns, but Gabe was sure, grinning at the thought, that if he had the time he could worm his way toward them through the tall grass until he could look into their dark liquid eyes.

Still, no self-respecting hunter worth his powder would pass up meat for his party. He would trespass lightly in this sanctuary, but already his mouth was watering for the tender rib meat dripping with red-brown juices. Nothing was as good as buffalo meat, not even this cow meat the white men bragged about. As the mountain men said, buffalo was the real tobacco chew. Of course, hunting by himself was not nearly as much fun as a big hunt with the Indians; he wasn't riding bareback, the jaw rope in his teeth, legs clamped tightly around the pony's ribs, hands free to slip arrows into a strong bow. He'd miss the yells and dust and excitement, the danger, the feasting and dancing. Ho! what times he had had during a good hunting season!

In a grassy pocket formed by a horseshoe bend in the creek, Gabe saw a small band of buffalo cows and calves. Immediately he turned Tibo toward the willows where he would be well screened. He stripped down to his breechcloth, put his knife in his teeth, and unholstered the Winchester. The grass tickled his chest as he moved forward in a crouched position, stopped, studied his quarry, and crept a few more paces. He trod softly, hoped the throbbing of his heart would not drum across the meadow. He must take care lest the blackbirds feeding alongside the buffalo give him away by taking wing.

Closer.

Closer.

Suddenly he spat out the knife and held his nose to keep from sneezing.

He pressed on, feeling the sun burn the sweat off his back. He drew one leg forward slowly, balanced his weight on one foot, brought the other up. Again, again. Even as a small boy he had loved stealing close to wild game to spy on them. Later he had improved this skill so as to be a better hunter. Now he approached stealthily, with infinite patience, so that he need make only one clean shot, and the stillness shattered briefly could enfold the valley quickly and the animals once more graze in peace.

Ah, there was his target, a fat young cow. He crouched, sat, steadied his elbows on his knees. He took careful aim along the level of the grass tops.

The hammer clicked; he squeezed the trigger. The cows spun around, bawling to their calves, and raced away. The sound of his shot echoed back over his head. Rising slowly, he looked around and saw that the meadow as far as he could see was deserted and the only movement that of grass rippling in the breeze and the afternoon clouds drifting toward him. A dark hump on the grass was all that remained to show that a hunter had intruded here.

He went to work with his knife, swiftly, expertly, struggling with the heavy carcass, the smell of the rancid, greasy wool strong in his nostrils. More than an hour of concentrated labor passed before he had the meat ready for the sack and had bathed quickly in the creek before turning back to Tibo.

The sun was slipping behind the tall pines on the lakeshore when he rode into camp. For a moment it seemed as if the whole world stretched before him in serene blue water, but his attention was diverted by the wrangler and Nute claiming the meat. Bean thumped him joyfully for his success. "No chores for you till after supper. Unsaddle that pony and wet your whistle in the lake. We'll put the ribs to cookin' proper."

Gabe unbuckled the cinch strap and yanked the saddle off Tibo. The pinto sprang away even before the saddle blanket slipped from his flanks. With a whoop Gabe galloped after him across the beach. His shirt was off before he reached the water, and in two quick wriggles he was naked and prancing, knees high, into the lake.

Brrrr! the water was icy and took away his breath. He jumped, ducked, rolled, belly-dived, and cuffed water over Tibo until he was blue and shivering and had to jump out. Then he whistled at Tibo, and the two raced along the shore until Gabe was winded from shouting at the gulls and pelicans. He came upon Judge Hedges with his pants rolled up, exposing white broomstick-thin legs, hauling in fighting, flashing trout. "Golly, two on one line!" Gabe gasped admiringly.

"Hungriest trout in Christendom!" Hedges exclaimed. "They'll snap at anything. This is a dry fly fisherman's paradise." When he bent to release the hooks, bold gulls screamed and circled over him until he tossed one fish high in the air. They swooped on it and plummeted to the beach with the prize.

"Aren't you keeping any for supper?" Gabe asked, and then ducked as a heavy-winged pelican flapped over him.

"Caught sixty already," the Judge boasted as he cast again and immediately braced as two more trout struck savagely. He was grinning from ear to ear. "Saved the best for supper, but lots of them are wormy and good for nothing but the birds." When two more trout were writhing on the coarse sand he offered, "Want to try your luck?"

Gabe did and he didn't. There was too much to see. "Later," he answered. "Where're the others?"

The horses and mules had been turned loose and after frolicking in the water and rolling and scratching in the sand had settled down to feed on the nearby grass. "Langford spotted carnelians and agates in the sand, so he and Hauser and the General are gem hunting. Everts is taking

107

a nap. Jake and his pals are floundering back in the woods somewhere, hunting. I just hope none of their shots go wild in this direction."

"Didn't they get anything?" Gabe asked with ill-concealed satisfaction.

"How could they?" Hedges said disgustedly. But he grinned as he cast again; the feathered fly dropped lightly on the water, and immediately the line sang off his reel. "Say, young man, you're shivering. Better get dressed."

As soon as the sun had dropped behind the trees the temperature cooled noticeably. Gabe raced back and piled into his buckskins. Then he took time to look around. In the east the red stony thrust of the Absarokas, shod in pines, was already shadowed to timberline, but above, the granite peaks flamed with the sun's last rays. In the southeast and south, across the darkening water, mirror smooth save where trout dimpled the surface, were stolid stands of evergreen forest; southwest the red bony hump of a mountain reached into the lake, and behind it flamed three fiery arrows—the Tetons.

So this was where the Shoshones had camped before they were shunted off to alien reservations! In his mind Gabe could see the tepees set back under the open timber, the smoke from cookfires spiraling through the branches or seeping out to form an aromatic cloud blanket over the campsite. The children of long ago had romped in the water and chased gulls off the sandbars, even as he had. The squaws had fished and dried trout and pemmican against the long winter, had culled gooseberry and currant from the thickets, and lived the good life.

Far, far across the water, beyond the neighboring

mountains, his father had run his trap lines. Oh, to be a gull and soar on gray and white wings to his homeland!

As night banners unfurled in the eastern sky, the sun emblazoned them in red, orange and gold and held back the darkness. The air was full of a thousand emotion-provoking, memory-stirring smells—of forests and snow-banks and wet rock; of fish and fowl and musky water animals; of flowers, berries, and grass and—and braising buffalo ribs! Gabe jumped for joy, spun around, and made his moccasins sing across the sand.

He scorned the battered tin plate, the beans, gravy, and even the biscuits. With his knife he carved off a thick rib steak and then went off a little way by himself to squat, sitting on his heels in true mountain-man fashion, and licked the juices trickling down his hands before devouring the meat and sucking the bone until it was dry. Meanwhile unaware of the amused glances of his friends, he finally straightened, walked to the lake, cleaned his knife, and dried it on his sleeve; then he drank and washed his hands and face, scrubbing away the strings of grease that veined his forearms from wrist to elbow. He rose, sighed gustily, and patted his full, hard stomach. Now he saw that the torchlights of the Absaroka peaks were dimming, and as night's blanket stretched farther across the water, the stars came to life. But then human sounds began to intrude; he must help Nute with the chores.

While he was scouring a skillet, he could not help overhearing the men talking. After such a feast of buffalo, there should have been mountain-man talk. But no; he kept hearing the word "road" mentioned frequently, and listened: the men were asking Hauser if his bank could support a loan large enough to build a road up the river, past the canyon, and on to the lake. The possibility of a road so disturbed Gabe that his face paled.

"What's the matter, boy?" Nute asked. "Is you getting sick?"

Gabe shook his head, as if to shake off the bad news. "They're talking about putting a road in here!" No, not a road! Not a highway for wagons and people who would strip the forests, put cows on the good grass, and chop up the meadows with parceling fences!

Now it was Nute who shook his head in amazement. "Where you been? They been talking about a road ever since we all camped by the canyon. How come you never heard?"

He hadn't heard because he had deliberately shut his ears to human talk so he could listen to the Yellowstone. Now, just as his rifle shot had shattered the harmony of Pelican Valley, so the word "road" and its nightmare aftermath of intrusion, clutter, and land-grabbing shattered his contentment. He had envisioned a trail, blazed only for sharp eyes, so he could lead white men into the wonderland, but never a road! Not here, not in his Yellowstone!

Of course, he should have known. Why, Mr. Langford had told that reporter in Helena why the expedition must solve the mystery of the Yellowstone. And Gabe had overheard every word. But he'd been deaf to the threat because at the time he was obsessed with the idea of proving that Jim Bridger was no liar.

He listened with a sinking heart. So the road would come. He must accept the fact as fatalistically as the Shoshones had accepted the intrusion of the white settlers and with the same sorrow they had felt when forced to cede their hunting grounds. Stoically he swallowed his heartache and after chores walked alone to the lakeshore. The water was silvered with starlight and moonrise, the mountains loomed softly black on the horizon.

Soon Gabe heard footsteps crunching on the sand, and someone called, "You there, son?"

"Yes." His voice was hoarse.

"What's the matter?" asked the Judge in fatherly fashion.

Gabe meant to say nothing, but suddenly in his heartsickness he lashed out. All the bitterness he had inherited from the Shoshones poured forth, all his love of the Yellowstone came into his voice; he even bared the secret of the Yellowstone and ended bitterly, "Do you white men have to destroy everything in the mountains? Can't you leave even one place as Our Father Above made it? How would you like to be hunted and hunted until there was no place left for you but a bare mountaintop?"

The Judge heard him out, until his words dried up. Hedges said nothing for a long time, though now and then he murmured, "Hmmmm . . . hmmmm," as if he were asking a profound question whose answer escaped him. But when the others shouted from the crackling campfire, the Judge finally suggested, "We better join our friends."

"No!" Gabe cried out. He ran for his blankets and moved far up the shore line where he would hear no more of this road talk.

Though he fought against it at first, the lake soothed him. The wind soughing through the evergreens cooled his flushed cheeks; resentment faded, and he gave himself wholly to the call of the Yellowstone. As he lay on his back, his head propped on his hands, eyes fixed on the stars, he began to sense a high, soft humming. Building and fading, it rippled above him. Ayeeee, he knew what it was; the Shoshones often spoke of it. Only the very brave, or the very pure in heart, heard it, because it was the whispering of the Great Spirit, a good omen always, though he could not fathom the message.

Then he remembered Judge Hedges' telling him that there were no such things as spirits, evil ones, gentle ones, Great One—none at all.

He thought about this a long time. Maybe it wasn't the voice of a spirit; maybe it was only the wind thrumming lightly across the water. But was there any harm in believing what he cherished of his Shoshone heritage?

He pulled the blankets up around his chin and hollowed a place in the sand for his hips. The lullaby brought peace to his sorrowing heart, and he slept.

VIII

Lost!

THREE days later Gabe got lost.

The expedition had run into trouble attempting to circle the lake. While rounding the east shore a cold wind, driving rain clouds before it, whipped up five-foot waves and hurled them across the beach. General Washburn turned the line of riders and pack mules into the forest. There the riders found they must punch a trail through a heavy growth of lodgepole pine and snarled windfalls. If Hauser hadn't set the course by compass, they would have had no idea of direction. Their axes bit deep, timber splintered, the mules brayed, and the men voiced their exasperation; overhead the branches threshed wildly, and the wind keened through the treetops.

Judge Hedges and the elderly Everts, his glasses teetering on his nose, the black shawl drawn tightly over his head, tried to locate a more open trail. They became completely confounded in the dark, tangled woods and were lost ten minutes after losing sight of their companions.

"What will we do now?" asked Everts, the most helpless of the entire party.

Hedges fired three quick shots with his rifle.

A short distance away Washburn heard the distress call and fired an answering volley. The others kept shouting, "Here! Here we are!" until the two strays reappeared.

Because of this, Langford would not allow Gabe to roam ahead to hunt, so there was no fresh meat that night or the next. The best Nute could manage was a monotonous fare of beans, biscuits, oatmeal, and small servings of ham. Already the eggs, butter, bacon, and tinned fruits were used up. However, after checking their provisions Washburn and the wrangler felt that the expedition would get by with additions of game meat and trout, "providin' it don't take no more 'n four or five days to go around the lake," Bean advised. "An' you git the chance, you spring that boy Gabe loose from Langford's mollycoddlin' and let him hunt. He won't get lost."

Three days had passed in battling the woods and little progress made.

"I've had enough of this," the timid Trumbull fretted, the gloomy forest making him more nervous than usual. "We've been gone twenty-two days, and we must be several hundred miles from Helena. Can't we go back to the lake outlet and strike for home?"

But Washburn and Langford had "explorer's itch," they claimed good-naturedly and said they wanted to push on so as to be the first to map the shore line. The others were agreeable, providing they didn't encounter too much more difficulty.

Gabe welcomed going around the lake. The longer he could stay in the Yellowstone, the better. Besides, some of the men were saying Yellowstone Lake was the true headwaters of the river, and he knew this was not so. Jim Bridger had told him the river flowed *into* the lake from the southeast and that its source was far up in the mountains. Gabe thought about telling Washburn and Langford this, but decided it would be better if they learned it for themselves; then they'd *know*.

When Gabe thought of discovering the real headwaters, those first tricklings bubbling over rocks and across flower-painted meadowland, of seeing them growing, growing, of hearing the young creeklet's voice deepening, the lifeline flourishing until it could feed a vast lake, then thunder in two mighty cataracts and chew a deep yellow canyon, his heart pounded with excitement. He must see the birth of this great river!

He was delighted when the expedition suddenly broke from dark shade into bright sunlight and he saw the mile-wide marshland bordering the inlet where the river entered the lake. He grinned as he heard Langford say importantly, as if he were the first to discover it, "By Jove, it's the river! The lake isn't the true headwaters after all!"

"It's the river, all right," Jake grumbled, "and it'll be the devil to cross." He slammed his heels into his horse's sides and urged him onto the watery ground; in a few seconds the poor animal was floundering in mud. Those who had followed Jake turned back immediately, and after some difficulty Jake's horse regained firmer ground.

"Wait here, all of you, until I find a better place up-river to ford," the General ordered, and the word was passed down the line to the last soldier.

"Can I go with you?" Gabe asked eagerly. When the General nodded, the two strung out, the General in the lead, along a game trail that skirted the marshland. The sky darkened as ahead of them flock after flock of wild fowl rose with a great clatter of wings—geese, mallards, trumpeter swans, blue herons, whooping cranes, and grouse. On each side of the river timbered foothills tilted toward the sudden thrust of the encircling peaks. Gabe sensed rather than saw these, because much of the time he and Washburn were forced to worm their way through brush and around thick-trunked pines. Three miles upstream they found a sound, gravel-bottomed crossing.

"This will do," Washburn decided. "Let's turn back."

Gabe hesitated. "Could I scout ahead? We need some fresh meat."

Recalling the wrangler's advice, the General agreed but cautioned, "Don't you dare get lost, or friend Langford will raise a ruckus." After he turned his horse he shouted, "And don't you dare forget the meat. That's an order!"

Gabe touched his fingers to his headband in salute and, laughing, called back, "No, sir!"

After he and Tibo drank, they crossed the river and soon came to the brink of a deep, heavily timbered ravine. Since it was impossible to pass, Gabe scouted the gulch, knowing it would narrow eventually, enabling him to swing around the head of it. But soon even he became confused in the dense timber, and working back toward the river, which was split by an island, Gabe thought he was fording one, and then another, creek. It was slow going on the narrow trail, and he rode hunched over, his cheek brushing Tibo's mane, to avoid the sharp-needled over-hanging branches.

Suddenly a brown bear loomed ahead, but as soon as Tibo trumpeted a shrill neigh the bear scampered off in the brush. Gabe laughed; from the time the expedition had moved south of the Gardner River he had seen considerable bear sign—rotten logs turned over by bears rooting for mice and grubs, berry and wild onion patches dug up, and tree trunks raked to sharpen claws; but he had seen no bears, probably because they hunted the high meadows for the spring crop of fawns. Tibo fought the bit and tried to turn, but Gabe finally got him past the bear's trail.

Gabe had never seen such jumbled country. The ground pitched; there were boulders obstructing the path; the fallen timber was heaped in hopeless confusion, like a pile of broken arrows. Only where lightning or fire had burned openings did the sun's rays cut through the heavy shade, and only here did orange-speared paintbrush and purple fireweed bring bright splashes of color to the otherwise dark ground cover.

He didn't feel lonely; woodpeckers and sapsuckers ceased their busy hammering and eyed him; camprobber birds flitted ahead of him; he whistled at squirrels whisking from branch to branch; he saw where deer and elk had browsed on tender-leaved bushes. Yet at the same time he realized that this portion of the Yellowstone was a threat to the expedition, because if the path were this difficult all along the south shore it would take many days to reach the west side.

He pulled on the reins lightly, and Tibo stopped. What should he do? Keep on this meandering trail? Ho! What if it led over a mountain and out of the Yellowstone? That could happen. Bridger had told him the headwaters were such a jumble of peaks, timber, and ravines that even a crow needed a compass to cross! He sat quietly in the saddle, thinking hard. It might be a good idea to climb the nearest peak; then he would get a better idea of the lay of the land.

He chuckled, and Tibo moved forward; this time Gabe held to the deer trails that lead upward through larger pine and spruce. The air was cool, the smell of pine overpowering, and the trail slick with its cushioning of needles. Soon there were the waist-high, white-plumed candles of bear grass to light his way higher and higher. When he reached the timberline he dismounted, wound the reins securely over a windfall, and continued on foot over the rough granite. Only after two hours of strenuous climbing did he reach the summit.

He straightened, took a deep breath of the cold, thin air, and unconsciously raised his arms as if he were a bird alighting. But the chill wind whistled up his loose sleeves, and he shivered, more from excitement than cold, and hugged the damp buckskin around his ribs.

Far below he saw the vast blue body of Yellowstone Lake. The outline resembled a hand! The outlet at the north formed the wrist span, a bay in the west a misshapen thumb, and in the south watery fingers pointed deep between timbered ridges.

He realized immediately that much of the southern shore line promised tough going; the trees marched close-ranked to the water; there was little open beach. If Mr. Langford wanted to map the shore line, he would have to climb a mountain, maybe this one; Gabe would blaze the trees so his friend could find the way up here.

From the southeast finger, or bay, he traced the upward course of the Yellowstone River until he saw where the sun-dappled silver thread frayed into two strands, one curling southward out of sight around a mountain, the other thinning out eastward on the north flank of the same mountain.

The fork! That was his sign! The Yellowstone was born of two sturdy beginnings. And so was he!

When he was born the medicine man had given him his "sign," a Y formed of strong, supple willow to symbolize he was the son of mixed blood, of a mother and father who loved the mountain streams, as did willow, strong and yet supple, qualities a half-breed child would need to flourish in a changing world. Thereafter, from the time he could trace the sign in the dirt the Y had marked his few possessions—his child's bow and play-warrior's shield, his porcupine-quilled moccasins. He looked forward to the day when, after he had fasted and seen his vision, his grandfather, the chief, would paint the sign with blood and clay on his forehead. He had been proud of that sign until the foul-tongued ruffians at Bridger's post had made him ashamed of being a "breed." But now that he knew the Yellowstone's sign was the same as his, he felt his heart cleansed of shame, the tiny thorn of bitterness drawn out, and the wound healed.

But his joy gave way to a more sobering thought. The fork: Indian sign or nature's, man's or river's, he must be worthy of his sign, even as the Yellowstone, which from its two beginnings came together to form a strengthening, powerful, handsome river—and a happy river, too, or why would Our Father Above have painted its canyon yellow, the Shoshone color for joy and Giver of Life? The Yellowstone was this also, nurturing as it did a sanctuary for the untamed ones—the birds and animals and until recently the Indians who sought the lake during the summer and fall.

If only the Yellowstone could always be a sanctuary, a refuge for wild animals! If only there was some way to hold back the hunter. Ho! what a dream! Gabe closed his eyes against the sunlight and prayed for a message, the message of the sign—of the Yellowstone. But it escaped him, and he knew why. He had not fasted or thirsted enough, or withdrawn in solitude, as was necessary. Although in his mind he strove to pull the very message from the wind and sky, it eluded him. It was not yet time. . . . He must wait. . . .

Meanwhile he need not be sad. No one could remain so on such a fine day, atop a mountain, with the blue sky overhead and the wind tantalizing him with the smell of snow and lichened rock and pine. Beyond the forks of the Yellowstone were the peaks where Bridger and his father had trapped and beyond them the Tetons, his homeland. He saw that it would take many days to reach the actual headwaters, that he could not hope to find the remote lake or spring from whence the great river first issued. No matter; he could try again. Meantime he had seen the sign; he had looked over the near beginnings; he was content.

He began turning slowly, gripping his toes on the rocks to steady himself against the buffeting wind. Yes, there were the Wind River Mountains to the east and the Absarokas and ragged-edged Beartooth to the northeast. He slipped off his headband and raked his fingers through his hair, lifting the long locks so the wind cut clean and cold across his scalp. He felt so good and warm deep down inside, even if he was shivering on the outside. Slowly the conviction grew in him, he could *feel* it growing, that his future and that of the Yellowstone were slowly tightening into one strand, even as green strips of rawhide could be wound and in aging grow strong and inseparable.

Since it was well past midday, he took one last look before groping his way down to timberline. Tibo greeted him with a shrill neigh and demanded to be petted and talked to before he would stop his playful nipping. About an hour later the two were well down the mountainside, and a sweet smell drew them to a patch of huckleberries. Dismounting, Gabe dropped to his knees and raked the tiny purple-blue berries from their short stems. When he was stuffed, he wiped his sticky, stained fingers on leaves and his mouth on his sleeve and leaped into the saddle.

He pressed on until twilight darkened the forest. Not until then did he come upon a trail where freshly disturbed earth indicated that the pack train must have passed. He urged Tibo to a faster pace, but realized in time that instead of going downhill toward the lake, he was climbing once more. It was so dark that he dismounted, took out his flint, and built a small twig fire and in the light of it discovered he had been following the trail of an elk herd.

Now what was he to do? He could blunder on in the dark; he really owed it to his friends to try and find the camp. But caution argued against this foolhardy action.

Suddenly he laughed out loud. He had wanted to be alone in the woods, and this was his chance. His stomach protested, but he ignored hunger. Happily he cleared a small place under the sheltering boughs of a large spruce. Close by where there was browse for the pinto he looped the reins over a low limb and took off the saddle and blanket. Then, burrowing in the soft duff of pine needles, he curled up in the blanket, his head on the saddle, and went to sleep.

He wakened to the sound of blood-curdling yells. He heard Tibo scream in fright, snap the reins, and bolt off down the trail.

The unearthly shrieks rent the air again.

Mountain lion!

Fumbling in the dark, Gabe scrambled up the tree under which he had been sleeping. He scraped his hands and legs, banged his head, tore his leggings, but ignored everything in his haste to get as far above ground as possible.

Seconds later the big cat, which he could not see but could hear growling and snuffling, closed in on the spruce. With a wild snarl it pounced on the man-scented blanket and saddle and ripped them to shreds. Then it began a frenzied circling, shrieking its rage at finding no quarry. Gabe didn't know whether to climb higher or remain absolutely quiet. He decided not to lure the killer by making any noise, but wasn't sure that his hammering heart wouldn't betray him.

Once the animal got the scent of the pinto, it tore at the bushes and clawed the windfalls. Now Gabe was frightened for Tibo's sake. He had to save the pinto! If the mountain lion found its trail, the little horse would be doomed.

The next time the lion screamed, Gabe screamed back. For a moment the cat was silent, then he heard its claws scraping up the tree trunk. He forgot about being quiet and climbed higher. Raging, the cat started after him. Even as Gabe groped frantically, lifting himself from branch to branch, he could hear the cat scratching its way up the trunk; he could see in his mind one razor-clawed paw, and then the other, reaching for him.

Cr-ack!

A limb splintered. The cat dropped to the ground, snarled, and once more began climbing. But after tearing at the bark a few feet, it gave up. Gabe heard it drop and bound off through the brush.

He sagged with relief against the rough tree trunk. Although thankful to be unharmed, he soon discovered the discomforts of his perch. Bristling needles and sharp scales stabbed through the buckskins. It was cold; his hands were gummy with pitch, his scratches smarting and bleeding, yet he dared not return to the ground before daybreak.

The night seemed a million years long. When at last he dared descend, he found every movement painful. He was stiff, racked with chills, and so hungry his head swam. He stamped around until he had limbered up enough to be able to carry the rifle and what was left of the saddle and blanket. Knowing the direction of the lake, he left the trail, struck diagonally across country, crossed the river, and soon came out on the shore of the southeast bay.

Water! He dropped his burden and ran to the lake.

After drinking slowly and washing his face and hands, he looked around. Not a quarter mile away, a fire blazed merrily on the beach. He scooped up his belongings and ran toward camp, calling loudly to his friends. Immediately he was smothered with backslaps, and was soon warming himself by the fire, wolfing a bowl of oatmeal. While he curled his fingers around a mug of coffee, Mr. Langford told him, "I thought you were with Judge Hedges and Stickney. They got lost, too, and didn't find our camp until nightfall. When you weren't with them, and the pinto wandered in minus its rider, I was mighty concerned."

General Washburn winked at Gabe. "I knew you weren't really lost. I told Langford you'd turn up in the morning."

Gabe did some quick thinking. He would never admit he had been lost. So he said stoutly, "Shucks, I warn't lost. I knew where I was every minute." Then he told them about the mountain lion and apologized to the wrangler for the saddle and blanket being ruined.

"I kin patch the saddle," Bean told him. "A saddle's a lot easier to replace than a boy."

Gabe grinned. Gosh, everyone made him feel so important. He'd been missed!

The Judge shivered. "I didn't like being out in the dark. I don't see how you stood it."

"Oh, it wasn't too bad," Gabe remarked, now that he was warm and fed.

When he reported what he had seen from the mountain-top and the trail he had blazed, Langford and Lieutenant Doane left immediately to make the climb so they could map the shore line, and the General asked Gabe to ride ahead with him. The going was so tedious that by mid-afternoon they stopped in a small meadow not far from the south finger of the lake. "It's hardly big enough to swing a cat in," the General remarked, "but we'd best go no farther. I'll wager our friends will be exhausted getting just this far."

Gabe's stomach turned over when he heard the word "cat"; he'd be a long time forgetting that experience. But after cutting firewood, he did not hesitate to go hunting and shot a young bull elk not five hundred yards above camp. By the time the pack train arrived the ribs were braising over hot coals.

Langford and Lieutenant Doane returned at dusk, en-thusiastic over the map they had sketched from the mountaintop. Langford was also excited about a large herd of elk in an alpine park and a fair-sized band of mountain sheep feeding on an adjoining mountain he had spotted with his binoculars. "What a hunter's paradise!" he exclaimed. "Wait till we tell the boys in Helena. They'll come swarming in here!"

Gabe felt every one of Langford's words hammer on his heart. The poor animals! Soon they would be driven from their feeding grounds and fall victim to hunters who shot, not out of necessity, but to brag about the size of their kill. To them, good hunting meant so many trophy heads, so many buffalo tongues, and a pack train staggering under spoiling carcasses. And if the word got out about there being good hunting in the Yellowstone, then the cold-blooded hunters who supplied the meat stores in the nearby towns with elk, deer, antelope, moose, bear, and mountain sheep would move in. Ayeeee, what a slaughter! And no one to make them hold back their deadly fire.

But Gabe had little time to mourn. He hopped from one chore to another, and later, while pouring a second round of coffee, he had a shock. He said nothing until he had looked around carefully, particularly in each tent, for the black-shawled, quiet Mr. Everts. Judge Hedges, noting the distressed look on Gabe's face, asked, "What's wrong?"

"I don't see Mr. Everts anywhere. Wasn't he with you today?"

The Judge couldn't remember when he had last seen Mr. Everts. Much of the day had been spent lifting the animals over windfalls or winding around them. He alerted the others, and immediately they began shouting Everts' name and firing their rifles. But there was no answering signal from the missing man. Lighting brands, Gabe and Langford searched back along the trail for several miles, calling every few seconds, then listening until their ears ached for the answer that never came.

"I wouldn't worry too much," Hauser advised when they stumbled wearily into camp. "I bet the old boy has decided to stay put until daylight. He'll turn up in the morning, like Gabe did."

Gabe hated to think of nice old Mr. Everts being all alone in the woods. The cat could still be prowling around. However, since there was nothing more to be done, and the others had gone to bed, he cut extra firewood and between naps kept one fire burning brightly all night in camp and another on the lakeshore.

All the next day and the next the men fanned out in

every direction, blazing trails, searching, but finding no trace of the missing man. Gabe grew more and more worried. Remembering the mountain lion, he did not spare himself searching for the old one. About midday, he noticed how still the forest was. No! not a storm coming, not now.

After chores that evening, he walked to the lake. There was a different raw smell in the air, the breath of the coming storm. The sky was black and starless, the lake motionless, save for the splash of a muskrat slipping into the water or a trout breaking the surface. From far in the forest the hoot owl called and was answered by the heron's eerie cry. When the damp cold pressed down on his shoulders, Gabe returned to camp. He cut extra firewood, saw to it that the pinto was in a sheltered spot, then worked fast to fashion a brush wickiup of close-needled spruce branches, weaving layer upon layer to deflect the wind and moisture. Before he had finished a few flakes of snow began drifting down, big wet flakes that hissed as the flames devoured them.

Poor Mr. Everts. . . .

Mr. Langford insisted Gabe sleep in his tent, but Gabe assured him he would be fine in the wickiup. Soon the snow was coming down so fast that everyone ducked for cover. Gabe crawled in the wickiup, pulled branches over the opening, and wriggled under his blankets, the rifle at his side, his coat over his shoulders. Soon he was warm and slept. But later he wakened and covered his head because the cold was bitter and the wind was tearing at the trees.

Poor Mr. Everts. . . .

Gabe knew well these first fall storms; they lasted sev-

127

eral days and left the ground blanketed with sopping, slushy snow. Neither man nor beast nor fowl stirred until the white threat had vanished. Golden warm days would follow, but before that Gabe was sure that Mr. Everts would be dead.

The dark, the cold, the isolation of the wickiup, the storm, the sad thoughts about Mr. Everts, all pressed in on Gabe; the Indian in him sought the meaning of it all. He thought and thought, dozed, dreamed, had nightmares in which Mr. Everts was pursued by the mountain lion and Gabe could not save him. He wakened, shivering, struggled to clear his mind, and burrowed deeper into his covers, shrinking against the piercing cold.

He thought harder and bit by bit began to see a pattern: the storm meant endurance, for he would be cold and hungry before it abated—thirsty, too, if he refused to wet his mouth with snow. The wickiup meant isolation, the aloneness he needed for prayer and seeking the message, the vision; the darkness and wind would keep his ears and the eyes of his mind from being distracted, so he might concentrate. . . . But what about morning, when he must work at chores?

Oh, message! Come quickly!

He need not have worried about morning. The storm kept everyone under cover; there was no fire building, no cooking, no one stirring or calling his name.

Gabe withdrew more and more into himself, remaining motionless despite the cold, feeling knots cramp his legs; he dreamed, wakened, dreamed again, this time of Mr. Everts being safe and warm in a hot springs basin.

Then nightmares took over again, dreams in which white men tried to strip the forests, but the steep trails discouraged them; others tried to build a road and cabins, and the Yellowstone's wintry blast drove them back. But then with terrible clarity he saw in his dream the hunters coming in, hordes of them, with snarling guns; the wild game fled in terror to the highest, barren peak where they bleated piteously for help, "Hold back the hunter! Hold back the hunter!" Gabe answered their call; brandishing a "spirit" fork, he drove the hunters back, back, back, until the sound of their gunfire faded and the wild ones once more flourished in nature's sanctuary.

Then that tableau vanished in swirls of yellow clouds, and he wakened and found he was trembling. Ayeeee, what a vision, what a message! He was to be the defender of the Yellowstone! His chest swelled, his blood throbbed in his veins and warmed him; he felt his strength gathering for the task. If only he could go now to the medicine man and, standing before the circle of warriors, tell of this wondrous vision.

Then his spine slackened, and he was cold again. There was no medicine man, no warriors—only white men who would tell him he had had no vision, that the message was only wild imagining brought on by cold and hunger.

Maybe they were right. Maybe he had dreamed of himself as defender of the Yellowstone because he ached to have the wildlife sanctuary protected from the hunters. Sorrowfully he realized that no man could bring this about, no more hold back the flood of hunters than he could stem the river's mighty torrent.

No! his heart protested. Hold fast to the message. It was real. Some day he would stand up against the hunters. He must not doubt that. Patience . . . patience. . . .

But patience could be as galling as rawhide thongs biting deep into the bound arms and legs of a captive. He felt hamstrung by his youth, his aloneness.

He heard his name called and recognized Mr. Langford's voice. He sat up, hugging his dream close, and rubbed the hope and yearning from his face; then he crawled through the opening. There was little time for thinking during the next three days. He had to help clear knee-deep snow from the cook area and start the fires, chop wood, tend the horses, hunt, and help in the fruitless search for the missing man.

He was shocked by the change in his friends. The loss of Everts, the storm, and skimpy food—all showed markedly on them, even on the usually optimistic Langford. Grieving for his friend, Hauser no longer looked fierce. Judge Hedges was sad; the General never ceased coughing. Walter Trumbull was so depressed that he acted queerly; even Jake and his friends lacked the energy to grumble. Gabe felt especially sorry for Nute; the Negro really suffered from the cold; hugging Booby didn't help any, so Gabe saw to it there was plenty of wood for a hot fire. Only the soldiers, toughened by field campaigns, seemed to be in good condition. The horses and mules had benefited by the rest, and once the storm passed, snatched at every green leaf within reach, so Gabe and Bean were forever moving them to better feeding grounds.

Since the vision, Gabe felt tall and skinny, but strong. He decided every man ought to have either some Indian in him or regular doses of mountain living; it gave him the staying power that city life had sucked out of these businessmen.

130

On the fourth day Gabe stood quietly in the circle of men as they faced a heartbreaking decision. "We've got to move on," General Washburn voiced their thoughts. "We're dangerously low on food. If we keep on searching, we might be trapped in another storm and —and never get out of here alive. I think we all agree that our friend perished during the storm."

The men nodded glumly, all but Gabe who stoutly believed in his dream that Mr. Everts had survived the storm by huddling near the warm springs and would eventually work his way out of the tangled wilderness. But he said nothing. Who would believe him?

The expedition battled its way to the western thumb of the lake, topped a difficult ridge, and turned north to intercept the Madison River, where a grassy valley and ranches promised easier travel and food.

Gabe was a little disappointed. He knew he was on his way out of the Yellowstone, with so many questions still unanswered. But he had a greater respect for the Yellowstone now; it was mighty tough. Furthermore, he had had his vision and had understood the message.

But how could he make the dream come true?

IX

The Greatest Wonder of All

GABE and Langford knew from what Jim Bridger had told them that they would come first to a tributary of the Madison River and must follow it northward, downriver, to the larger stream. Once more the perverse country fought them with every difficulty imaginable—steep ascents, dense and tangled timber, bogs, cold, and rain.

What was the Yellowstone trying to keep them from this time? Gabe pondered as the rain trickled down his neck. Did it mean to defeat them with fatigue and starvation as the price for invading its sanctuary? Hadn't they paid enough in sweat and strain? Or was this just a further testing of his own endurance and faith? Well, the others might drag and falter and fret; he would not weaken.

Walter Trumbull asked querulously time and again, "What day is it? Are you sure we aren't lost? You're positive we'll find the Madison?"

On this morning, as on all others, Langford answered confidently, "We are not lost. We are going in the right direction. Today is Sunday, Walter, September eighteenth. We'll be home shortly."

"Shortly!" Jake snorted, the bad weather having failed to dull his tongue. "It took us thirteen days to go around the lake. We won't get home for a month, if then."

"Oh, shut your infernal mouth!" Hauser exploded.

Gabe held his breath, certain that there'd be a real squabble this time. But Jake shrugged, and the danger passed.

During the morning's ride, as the horses slipped and stumbled on the slick forest cover, all but Gabe and Langford rode slump-shouldered and dejected. Finally the rain slackened, and there was a noticeable lightening of the forest gloom. When the expedition lunched in a small clearing, Gabe studied the sky. The cloud layer was thinning; before too long the sun would appear. Filling the General's mug with coffee, Gabe saw how gaunt and tired he looked and tried to cheer him by commenting, "Good weather coming up."

Washburn's hand was shaking so that he had difficulty holding the mug steady, and he coughed repeatedly. "I hope so!"

"We got some open country ahead of us, even before we reach the Madison. That'll help," Gabe added, remembering that Bridger had told him, "Ye'll turn your back on the Yellowstone once you top the ridge west of the lake; but don't fret. There be an eye-popper or two left to make a lad jump out of his moccasins, on the Firehole, that is. You'll foller it north to the Madison, and then skeedaddle easy over the grass to Virginia City."

133

An eye-popper or two. . . . What could that mean? Excitement stirred in Gabe. Bridger wouldn't tell him more; he insisted it would spoil the fun. Did he mean the glass mountain? Or the pool with the fire burning in the bottom? He'd heard Langford tell the men that there were hot springs strung out along the Firehole. Gosh, maybe there was another Dragon's Mouth. He grinned at the thought. It was about time the Yellowstone came up with another laugh or two.

After the unappetizing midday meal of warmed-over beans and coffee, the expedition strung out again. Soon the evergreens were more widely spaced, and the ground leveled off so that the pack animals quickened their pace. Also, there were fewer windfalls snarling their way and many more birds than in the somber forest of the southernmost lakeshore. Before long the riders found their way blocked by a shallow canyon where a stream cascaded over a series of hundred-foot falls. Langford wanted to stop and explore a bit, but the others refused. Washburn, on being told this was the Firehole River, turned onto a game trail that followed the bank northward. Scarcely more than a mile farther the forest ended abruptly, and the riders found themselves on the rim of a large, treeless thermal basin. The cloud cover, driven by a steady breeze, tore apart, drenching them with hot sunshine. The dazzling light, coming so quickly after the deep shade of the woods, momentarily blinded everyone.

While rubbing his smarting eyes, Gabe heard a throaty muffled roar close by. Tibo immediately flicked his ears back and forth and grew restless. The roar subsided, but mushroomed again and then exploded with a thunderous "wh-oosh!" Gabe blinked rapidly to clear his sight, just

134

in time to see a tremendous shaft of boiling water rocket skyward and climb up and up and *up*, until a banner of diamond-bright crystals floated from the crest; then steam clouds boiled hundreds of feet above that. Tibo reared, but Gabe fought him to a standstill without taking his eyes off the unbelievable sight: a column of water jetting nearly two hundred feet in the air, while thousands of gallons in sparkling droplets and spray plummeted groundward, splashed over a wide area, and drained away through a network of threadlike tricklings.

Then before Gabe and the others could recover from their amazement, smaller geysers nearby began to gush and gurgle and lift white-hot streamers skyward in flash after flash of steam; hot springs boiled, steam vents puffed, the whole basin broke out in a watery ballet. But the great geyser, erupting from its broad, solitary cone, claimed their attention once again by the sheer glory and magnificence of its performance. After about a four-minute eruption, it receded gracefully in diminishing spurts until only wisps of steam curled from its throat.

So hypnotized that he was almost witless, Gabe recovered when memory served him. With the first glad whoop to cross his lips in days, he exclaimed, "That's the water spout Bridger said spouted higher 'n a flagpole!" But his words were drowned out by the others cheering lustily as the horses pranced on the whitened crust.

"Let's look down the hole!" Gabe suggested, jumping to the ground and flipping the reins around the nearest tree. Even as he raced toward the geyser, his moccasins singing on the sandlike burnt ground, he could hear the others at his heels. The mouth or orifice of the geyser, about four feet wide, was centered in a vast mound of geyserite, gray-white hydrous silicate deposited over thousands of years to form a tough, deep crust. Dropping down on his hands and knees, he cautiously peered into the opening. The breath of the geyser smelled mostly of hot mineral water, with a suggestion of the disagreeable rotten egg odor. He saw that the tube was beaded and dark yellow, and he could hear water gurgling far, far below.

By this time the entire mouth was ringed with his excited companions.

"Never seen *any*thing like it!"

"Most wonderful sight in the whole world!"

"Beats anything we've seen so far!"

"Dad-blame show-off, it's a circus all by itself."

"How soon will it erupt again?"

"No way of knowing."

Langford sat back on his heels. "Anybody got any idea what to call this thing? I suppose we ought to give Bridger some credit for telling the truth about it, but I'll be hornswoggled to know how you can fit that into naming a geyser."

"Call it Bridger's Geyser; the old boy is always spouting and running off at the mouth," Jake wisecracked, only to discover his joke fell flat.

None of the others could dredge up any suggestions. Fatigue and depression forgotten, they got to their feet, tipped back their weather-beaten hats, and scratched their heads, but even this didn't help stir up any new ideas. Shading their eyes, they looked out over the basin that bordered each side of the Firehole River in its bow-shaped west and northward course. From the riverbank

136

to the encircling timbered ridges there were countless steaming pools, spouters, and smaller geysers in play.

The big geyser was not only isolated at the southernmost tip of the bow, but dominated the entire scene because of its vast mound of gray-white geyserite. "As long as it sort of looks out over everything, what about calling it the Guardian—the Guardian of the Valley?" Langford suggested.

Gabe wrinkled his nose. That wasn't half exciting enough.

"Agh, you'll have to think of something better than that," Hauser remarked, but when pressed for another name he said he was so rattled he couldn't even think.

General Washburn listened at the rim of the tube. "It doesn't sound like it's going to erupt any more. I read somewhere that most big geysers don't play very often, some only every year or so. We had phenomenal luck seeing this one perform."

Hedge's face had the look of a small boy about to start a foot race. "Maybe we better explore before the sun goes down. This is no place to wander around after dark."

Washburn looked hopefully at each man. "Are you willing to take the time? It means not reaching the Madison tonight."

When they all nodded enthusiastically, Hauser checked his badly tarnished watch and said, "It's only three o'clock. That gives us several hours of daylight."

"Who cares about time now?" the Judge said, chuckling.

"I do," Jake announced. "When do we eat?"

Langford tore his hair in mock despair. "Great God in

Heaven His wonders doth reveal! And all Jake can think about is his stomach!"

Washburn jumped to his feet. "How about splitting up, some to search on one side of the river and some the other?" Forgetting his former fatigue and drawn by the sight of a sputtering spring, he trotted off to ford the narrow, shallow river.

As the men scattered, the soldiers prepared to make their camp, and the wranglers and Nute headed for the timber to search for a fresh-water spring. Gabe looked longingly at Washburn, then turned dutifully after Elwyn Bean. But the bewhiskered wrangler said, "G'wan, get the geezers outa yore system. You're too plumb addlepated to swing an axe. You can do your chores after supper."

With a yelp Gabe dashed to catch up with Washburn and Langford, who had paused to take off their worn boots and socks before crossing the Firehole. Gabe kicked off his moccasins, stuffed them under his knife sheath, and waded out. He stepped gingerly over the graveled bottom, feeling the icy water cut like a knife across the back of his legs. Midstream he stopped, a puzzled look on his face.

"What's the matter?" Langford called to him.

Gabe lifted one foot and then the other. "The water's cold, b-but it's hot on the bottom!" Then he gasped, his eyes widened, and he flapped his arms and jumped up and down. "Hey, this is the river that's cold on top and hot on the bottom! I found it, I found it! Jim weren't lying after all." He cavorted around, not caring how wet he got, laughter pouring from him in breathless spurts.

The general waded out. "Well, I'll be!" he exclaimed, his gaunt face radiant.

Langford poked around with his feet. "There must be some warm seepage along here, probably from underground hot springs. That's why the water is warm below but cold on top." Even he threw back his head and laughed. "This is one story I never expected to be true. I thought for sure Bridger was pulling a whizzer."

Gabe quieted, blissfully feeling the warm water bubble through his toes and the cold water numbing his legs. But when he saw a small geyser lift a shaft of water thirty feet in the air, he crossed the river and ran toward it. He stuck his toe in the overflow seeping over the beaded edge of the pool and then hopped around on one foot, the smarting toe in his hands. As Washburn and Langford came up, their boot strings dangling, still another geyser began playing, first with a high-pitched hissing, followed by a sw-oosh that rocketed a stream over two hundred feet high. Because they were too close, a shower of boiling droplets rained down over them. "Ayeeee!" Gabe yelled and fled to a safe distance. As the scalding spray peppered his buckskins, he felt as if he were being attacked by a swarm of bees.

This perpendicular jet issued from a small cone about three feet high. "You'd never take that for a geyser," Washburn remarked. "It looks more like a beehive."

"Beehive is right," Gabe answered, shaking the buckskin shirt to cool his stinging shoulders.

"I think I'll take notes on these geysers so we won't be confused later on." Langford hauled out a grubby piece of paper and pencil stub. "When we start telling the folks in Helena about these, we better have the facts or we'll be called liars."

Gabe fidgeted while Langford wrote down *Beehive* and described its shape, noted its approximate location in the basin, and estimated its height of eruption. When he mentioned he might as well add notes on the Guardian, as he called the great geyser for lack of another name, Gabe couldn't stand still another second, nor could Washburn. The two galloped from one hot spring to another, past thumping steam vents, one that whistled like a tea kettle, another that growled something like the mountain lion that had treed Gabe, and still another that had a chimney-shaped cone.

"Hey, there's smoke coming out of the chimney!" Gabe chortled, but darted on to see others.

Langford caught up with them, and the three spent almost an hour combing the area, discovering one fantastic pool or geyser after another: a geyser that sloshed water like a butter churn; a purple-gray pool; another like an inkwell; pools whose edges showed splotches of green, yellow, or pink, each color intensified by the reflections of late afternoon sunlight.

Gabe happened to look back, southward, and blurted, "That big one's going to pop again!"

A great belch of steam poured from the orifice; then followed several jets of water, each pushing a little higher, and next a cannonading roar that made the ground tremble before the huge tower of water climbed skyward, held its peak for several minutes, then slowly subsided until only steam writhed from the opening.

Langford checked his watch. "It's been only an hour since we saw it erupt the first time. What a show!"

"Marvelous, sim-ply marvelous. Unbelievable," murmured Washburn.

They moved on, and when Hauser shouted to them from across the river, they waded over and joined him and Hedges. Hauser pointed to a jagged cone that he said reminded him of the Roman Colosseum and hastened to examine it more closely; but just then the geyser grumbled, the ground shook, and everyone fled when a gigantic pillar of boiling water erupted to a height of over two hundred feet in the air. They watched and watched it and were joined by Jake, Trumbull, Stickney and Gillette; then they all watched it some more, their ears full of its thunder. Hauser timed the eruption and after a bit said, "Fif-teen minutes! And no sign of lessening. I'll bet a million gallons of water has erupted so far."

After a second quarter hour, Hauser protested, "My watch must have run down. No geyser in the world could play that long."

"But it has, a whole half hour," Langford insisted, looking at his watch. When a third quarter-hour passed with no subsidence whatever and a hundred small rivers poured off the mound, Hauser shook his fist at it. "Dad blame you, stop spouting! D'you want to make a liar out of me?" He turned his back on it, and stamped toward the campsite.

Since the sun had dropped behind the trees, the others trailed him. The Giant, as they named it, had them absolutely bewildered with its power and majesty.

Nute greeted them with good news. "Meat for suppah!" The soldiers had had good luck hunting, and there were antelope, geese, and venison aplenty. With a little flour and fat for biscuits, the Negro had prepared a festive meal.

While they sat cross-legged on the ground to eat, the Guardian erupted again, and again an hour later, and again, maintaining its hourly schedule through twilight and into darkness. Gabe unrolled his blankets on the open ground so he could hear more of the music of the geyser basin. All about him was the merriest splashing and gurgling, the light voice of the river, the singing of the evergreens. He sniffed the ground; yes, it smelled burned, age-old burned; the geyser water had an indescribable odor, one that hinted at tremendous depths, of fires burning far in the bowels of the earth. Yet there was nothing frightening here, no need to hold his nose as he had at the Dragon's Mouth. Here all was happy and full of life.

Through the night the Guardian played again and again, and each time Gabe wakened and watched the ghostly pillar soar against a star-bright sky. What a friendly spirit it was! He became accustomed to its talk, the deep-throated gurgling, the triumphant roar as it reached its crest, the sighing as it subsided. The geyser became a personality for which he felt a growing affection.

He had been awed by the canyon and falls, rocked by the Dragon's Mouth, soothed by the lake, but this—! The Guardian made his heart beat faster, joyfully. It was an eye-popper, all right.

At dawn he watched the Guardian's boiling shaft and spray turn pink and yellow in the first rays of the sun, and he whooped when General Washburn asked the men, who agreed readily, to delay at least a few more hours in order to explore the geyser basin further. Jake's group held to the west shore of the Firehole and covered an area two miles back into the timber, where they found a Sapphire Pool, as they called it, numerous spouters, and biscuit-knobbed springs. Next they crossed uneven ground into another area where there were more surprises: a pool edged with black algae, another whose sides were rainbow-hued, still another pool—Emerald Pool, this time, quiet, clear, and startlingly green.

Gabe, Washburn, Langford, Hauser, and Hedges went north on the east side of the river; passed the Giant which was only puffing lazily; discovered and named Grotto Geyser, because of its arched, cavernous cone; Riverside Geyser, that shot an angry stream sidewise and almost horizontal to the river; and Fan Geyser, which scattered its spray in riblike jets that wavered in the breeze, like the opening and closing of a fan. Then Gabe ran on ahead, climbed a slight rise of ground, and found something so beautiful that he dropped on his stomach to view it. Below him, near the river, was a large, clear-purple-blue pool that reminded him of wild morning-glory. The fluted edge, the down-spiraling throat, the sun-golden petals—it was the most beautiful small thing he had ever seen. Soon his friends came along and knelt to marvel. Though Hauser, in a rare poetic frame of mind, thought it looked like a perpetual raindrop, the others, of one accord, called it Morning Glory Pool.

Meantime the Guardian repeated its performance, and Gabe, almost bursting with admiration, murmured, "Gosh, it hasn't failed us once. It's sure faithful."

Langford snapped his fingers. "Faithful. That's it. That describes it. Let's call it Faithful Geyser! No, wait . . . Old Faithful! That sounds even better."

"Old Faithful," Gabe repeated slowly, a smile crinkling his bronzed cheeks, the words pleasant on his tongue. "Yes, Old Faithful!" Then he added earnestly, "We can't leave Old Faithful without a proper salute." So he unholstered the Winchester and fired three shots rapidly, the others joining in with a ragged volley and cheers. Then Gabe hugged the rifle to his chest, lest he explode from holding in too much joy. Although he knew this was farewell to the Yellowstone, he was thankful that the very best the Yellowstone had to offer him had been saved for the last bright look.

X

A National Park . . .

THE expedition made excellent time along the narrow but open valley of the Firehole. Wherever possible
Gabe rode close to the river so he could see the countless
steam vents, pink and green mud pots, and jewel-toned
hot pools strung along its course. Under a cloudless sky
and bright sun, the steam danced in the light breeze and
sometimes whirled in long streamers through the nearby
lodgepole and spruce; frosted aspen lighted the somber
forest with the dry fire of yellow leaves; killdeer and bold
blue jays skimmed above the clear water. Over all lay the
subdued breath of the mineral springs and the sharper
scent of sage and pine.

No doubt about it; autumn had come on the heels of
the storm. Gabe saw it in the curling willow leaves and the
glowing red of wild rose thickets; he could hear autumn
in the blasting, rutting call of the elk, in the dry rustle of
aspen branches, and in the flocking songs of the birds;

145

he even tasted autumn in the winey, frost-blackened chokecherries.

Although this was the Firehole and not the Yellowstone drainage, Gabe thought of it as an inseparable part of the Yellowstone, the wonderland so different from any other mountain country he had roamed. He wished the men weren't so very anxious to return to Helena. He wasn't in any hurry; no one was worrying about whether or not he was alive. After all, he didn't have a real home, only a pallet in Jim Bridger's loft, and he came and went as he pleased and no questions asked. "I wish we could stay here till snowtime," he mentioned to Judge Hedges when they stopped later for coffee and cold biscuit.

But the Judge explained, "We've been gone four more than the thirty days we allowed for this outing, and it will be another week before we're actually home. Our families are probably worried sick."

Langford chuckled. "I bet that young whippersnapper of a reporter for the *Herald* is writing all sorts of scare headlines. He probably has us swallowed up in mud pots or eaten alive by the wild beasts."

Hauser grunted. "The sooner we get home and send a search party out for Everts, the better I'll feel."

"Amen to that. All the more reason to hurry," Hedges agreed. "I shudder to think of the court cases that must have piled up while I've been gone."

Stickney spoke up. "I've lost all track of time. What day is it anyway?"

"Monday, September nineteenth," Langford informed him.

The storekeeper groaned. "Oh, no! I haven't sent out my order for winter merchandise yet."

"Nor I," Gillette chimed in, "and if the bull teams don't bring in the flour before snow closes the roads, we'll have another flour riot." After a few moments he said wistfully, "But right now, I'll be danged if I care. What is it about this place? It does something to a man, makes him forget he has a care in the world. I couldn't worry, even if I wanted to."

"We better get to a town soon," General Washburn said, laughing when he wasn't coughing. "I don't think these trousers and boots of mine can hold out much longer." He tried to run his fingers through his tangled beard. "It'll take a barber two hours to make me look civilized." He drained his battered tin mug and waved it. "Gabe, how about another round?"

Gabe obliged and afterwards stretched out on the warm grass, his hands under his head, feeling the sun burn through the tears in his worn buckskins. A smile lifted the corners of his mouth. Even if he hadn't seen half the wonderful sights along the Firehole, he still got a prickly feeling whenever he thought about Old Faithful. The geyser basin had been more exciting than any Indian celebration; it wasn't hard to pretend the trees were shadowed tepees and the coyotes skulking around, the dogs in an Indian camp. Some of the vents thumped like drums, others smoked like campfires; the noisy spouters, the colored pools, the leaping waters, all reminded him of feathered, painted, yowling dancers. No wonder he felt so much at home.

The Yellowstone had been good to him. It had tested him and made him prove he had the makings of a real mountain man.

The Yellowstone had not betrayed him; no, sirreeee,

147

though there were many of Bridger's stories yet to be "authenticated," as Mr. Langford kept saying. No matter; he didn't need an excuse to return, but it was nice knowing there must be many more eye-poppers to lure a person back year after year.

He stretched, luxuriating in his contentment. Jim Bridger was no liar; the Yellowstone had proved that. He'd leave it to the others to tell the world that Jim's stories were not pure fiction; it would be his special thrill to tell that to the old pathfinder.

He wouldn't have missed the expedition for anything; not only for what he'd seen and done, but for the fun he'd had with Tibo and the friends he had made. Though he still had an uneasy feeling every time he thought about Mr. Everts. The nice old man simply had to turn up safe later on or, Gabe worried, his dream would have been all wrong. And if that dream was false, how was he to know if the big dream, the vision, was true?

But it had to be! After a man fasted and prayed, his vision seldom failed him if he was brave in heart. He had certainly tried hard to be that. Of course, sometimes it took years for a vision to be fulfilled; but right now, the closer he came to leaving the Yellowstone, the harder it was for him to see how to get a running start on making that vision come to life.

He sighed, rolled over on his stomach, and plucked at the grass. It was a problem indeed: how to hold back the hunter, when all his friends were talking about was how soon the road could be built and they could make money from the canyon and geysers.

Then why did I dream what I did, that I would hold back the hunters, if I can't make the dream come true?

he asked himself. His heart ached for the wild animals. Once the road was slashed through the timber and over the ridges, he bet there wouldn't be a single place where a man could stand right out in broad daylight and watch elk and deer and buffalo grazing, or beaver building their dams, or moose feeding in the ponds. After the first onslaught of hunters, the wild game would be afraid of man; they would have no peace. Once the guns started barking, they'd flee to the next ridge, and the next, only to see hunters closing in on them from every direction. There would be no more sanctuary for them in all these great stony mountains.

The sounds of the riders getting ready to move on made him push his worry far back in his mind. His friends were no longer in a dawdling mood. As soon as they drained their mugs, they yanked out the picket pins and called to each other, "Tonight we camp on the Madison!"

"And tomorrow night, or the next, it's good-by beans and bedrolls and hello to a tub bath and a barber and a hotel bed," Walter Trumbull gloated, coming more alive and less nervous with each mile, now that, as he put it, "Our ordeal is over."

Ordeal? Gabe snorted. He had his private opinion about that.

Hurry, hurry, hurry! Don't take time to explore a geyser basin ten miles north of Old Faithful; barely glance at a huge hot spring, over *four hundred* feet across; ride right past a turquoise pool, past more painted mud pots, past another hot spring that Gabe thought was on fire until Langford explained it only looked that way because of the gas bubbles breaking on its surface. Gabe was disappointed; he thought for sure he'd found the one

Bridger had said had a fire burning in it, until he remembered the fire was said to burn at the *bottom* of the pool.

The others rode on while Gabe and Langford tarried a moment at the "flaming" spring. Then Langford suggested, "Why don't we cut through the timber and see if we can't scare up some meat for supper? Jake will start banging away in another hour anyway, unless he and Gillette decide to race for the Madison."

Before long the two picked up good elk sign and followed a trail east of the Firehole. After winding through light timber for some distance they came upon a small thermal basin where a geyser was playing. Langford promptly called it the White Dome because of its conspicuous mound and took notes on it.

Gabe meandered around from one hot pool to another. Atop the pinto, he peered into the unusually deep blue depths of a steaming spring. Suddenly golden tongues of flame shot from below and erupted on the surface in gaseous bubbles. He couldn't believe his eyes and shouted for Langford, who came on the run. When more golden lights flickered in the depths, Langford gasped, "Why, it looks like there's a gas jet burning down in the bottom." Then the two looked at each other, whooped, and reached out to shake hands vigorously.

"Yahoooo!" Gabe shouted, and the sound echoed back from the foothills.

They had found the lake with the "fire" burning in the bottom.

Farther along they downed their elk and then turned westward toward the Firehole. Soon they emerged from the timber onto a broad meadow where the Firehole and another clear stream, rushing from the north, joined to form the Madison. Sheltered on the west by a handsome mountain, knee-deep in grass for comfortable sleeping and good grazing, it was the ideal campsite of the entire journey. Bean had the tents up already; the soldiers had their cookfire burning; the mules frolicked in the shallow water or rubbed their sweaty backs on the grass. Downstream Hedges was reeling in a fighting trout. Gabe chuckled. "I bet the Judge has caught a skillion trout this trip."

Nute was glad to have the elk meat. "Good thing we come to a ranch tomorrow," he told Gabe while they readied supper. "I had to turn the sacks inside out to get enough flour for biscuits and gravy. Mmmm-mmmmh! I plumb forgot how to cook proper, with eggs and butter."

"Anything you cook tastes swell to me," Gabe told him as he threw a morsel to Booby.

After a bit Elwyn Bean, the wrangler, drifted over to the cookfire. "Looks like the geyser basin'll be a right busy place next summer, the way Langford and his bunch are talkin'. Whether they git that road or not, folks is goin' to hanker to see them spouters." Gabe and Nute nodded as they turned the meat and stirred gravy. Bean cocked his head on one side. "I got the mules and campin' gear. Maybe us three could throw in together next year."

Nute banged the iron spoon on the rim of the kettle. "Don't talk to me about coming back heah! Too many things growling for me. Next job I have is working for a hotel, or a ranch. No more wilderness for me, thank you."

Gabe was wide-eyed. "Do you really mean it?" he asked Bean.

"I do," the wrangler said. "I been thinkin' you're a top

151

hand, and a hunter too. And seein' as how you know so much about this country, maybe you could do a little guidin' on the side."

"Honest?" Gabe was grinning from ear to ear. "I already made up my mind to come back, but I'd rather wrangle than wander around loose." His mind raced ahead, full of thrilling possibilities. After all, he did have to think about the future. "Golly, I could ask Bridger for a lot more information when I see him this winter, but I'd be back in Helena afore summer. You—you're not funning me?"

"I shore ain't," Bean assured him. "There's good money wrangling greenhorns, and they're a lot less trouble and more company than cattle. I'm sorry you're not interested, Nute, but I'd sure be glad to have you, Gabe. So think on it."

Gabe was so excited he almost let the meat burn. If he worked for Mr. Bean he could be a wrangler, *and* a hunter, *and* a guide! He'd thought a little about being a guide when he was older and more experienced; starting this early, he might end up as famous for guiding expeditions up the Yellowstone as Bridger was for leading emigrants over South Pass. Maybe he'd be known as Yellowstone Gabe or Yellowstone Kirkpatrick. No matter, he wouldn't worry about that; he'd earn the name first, like a warrior counting many coups.

During the entire meal and while he was helping with the clean-up, all Gabe could hear was talk about the road. When the men gathered around their campfire, Judge Hedges motioned him to sit beside him. "I'm going to say something you'll want to hear," he whispered, because by now Langford was moderating a friendly argument as to just how the Yellowstone could best be exploited for their personal profit.

"I still say we should file claims on quarter-sections around the canyon and lake and especially the geyser basin," Jake kept saying to override any other suggestions. "If we don't, some one else will, in another year or two. We should form a corporation and build our road and charge folks to use it, to view the canyon, or camp by the lake, or watch the geysers. It's that simple." He rubbed his hands together. "Once the road is paid for, we'll make us a tidy fortune."

"And you'll ruin the Yellowstone," Gabe wanted to protest, but as usual held his tongue. All this money talk was bleeding the joy out of him.

"Wouldn't there be a good side profit in cutting timber?" Stickney asked.

"I'll bet the butchers in Virginia City and Helena would buy all the meat you could bring out of here," Gillette suggested. "Buffalo is so scarce in these parts they'll pay a fancy price for it."

Suddenly General Washburn interrupted. "Cornelius," he began, using the Judge's first name, "you haven't said one word about all this. Don't you approve? It's time we heard from you. Speak up, man."

Gabe watched his friend as he got to his feet slowly and waited until every one was attentive. "I'm afraid you won't think much of what I'm going to say. But an idea has been taking shape in my mind ever since that first night we camped beside the lake. It's this: I don't think any one man, or any company of men, has the right to profit from the beauty wrought by God in this headwaters country. There ought to be no private ownership of

153

any part of this land. Must we exploit the Yellowstone? I would rather see us work unselfishly toward having this entire region set aside as some sort of refuge, a reserve for the use and enjoyment of all people . . . a sort of national park."

"A national park?"

"Where'd you get that idea?"

"Who ever heard of such a thing?"

"Yes, a national park," Hedges continued seriously, "one to be protected from all manner of exploitation so it can be enjoyed by generations to come; so the falls won't be harnessed by a dam, as some of you want; nor the timber slashed; nor the wildlife slaughtered. I don't mean the city park sort of thing, all grass and pansy beds; I mean a park that would always remain in its wild state, where you couldn't pick the flowers, or gather specimens, or deface the rims of those beautiful pools, or kill off the wildlife." He eyed his companions meaningfully. "You know what this place will look like after the loggers and hunters get through and the sections we don't file on are taken over by homesteaders."

The men looked away self-consciously. They knew.

"Oh, I don't think we have to worry too much about homesteaders," Hauser spoke up. "I think we all agree the Yellowstone is too high and broken up for ranching. It's the lumber barons who would wreck this place."

His friends nodded. They all had seen timbered mountainsides reduced to ugly wastelands by logging.

Gabe had hardly breathed since his friend had begun to speak. His mind was boiling with hope, with new ideas. Why, Hedge's idea was a way to make his vision come true!

General Washburn cleared his throat and tried not to cough as he said, "I think Cornelius is right. We white men have pretty much cut the West to pieces. I think it's high time we thought about something other than grabbing for ourselves. I like the idea of having one place left just as God made it, as a refuge for wildlife and a recreation area for all the people."

Refuge. . . . The word strummed a deep, joyful note in Gabe's heart. "Ooooh," he sighed longingly. He tried not to sound too thrilled. "Wouldn't that be wonderful? Then the elk and buffalo would have a place all their own, just like the Indians have their reservations. Could you really do that?"

One by one the men hearkened to the prayerful hope in his voice and the hunger and joy in his thin young face.

"Well, I don't know that we'd get anywhere, but it's worth a try. I'll work for a national park," Hauser put in.

"And give up the chance to make yourself a lot of money?" Jake argued.

"Yes," Gillette said.

"Yes," Stickney and Trumbull declared simultaneously.

Jake looked at them as if they had lost their wits.

"Yes," Gillette repeated the word firmly. "I'd like to come back here year after year and see the Yellowstone just as unspoiled as it is right now. As far as dollars and cents are concerned, I'm as hardheaded a businessman as you are, Jake, but I'll be hanged if I want to see this place ruined!"

"Nor I!" exclaimed Langford. "That's the most marvelous idea I ever heard of, Cornelius. I'm all for it, heart and soul!"

"Where would you start working toward a national park?" Hauser asked, his blue eyes blazing. "Do you think we could do it?" he asked Washburn, because the General was a prominent government official.

"I—I don't know," Washburn answered, looking quite doubtful. "It's a pretty revolutionary idea, and Congress is always so slow—but we certainly can try! As soon as we get back to Helena, we can write our Montana Territorial delegate, Mr. Clagett, to petition Congress to establish the country's first national park on the Upper Yellowstone. We're men of considerable influence out here; he'll do it. And if it means some of us have to go to Washington and help persuade Congress, will you all do your part?"

"You bet!"

"Sure!"

"Count on me!"

The General smiled at Jake. "You, too?"

The little man shrugged. "I think you're wasting your time and passing up a chance to make a lot of money. Maybe you'll change your minds after you all get back to Helena."

The General turned to Gabe, who looked as if he had seen the glory of heaven open up before him. "You'll help, won't you?"

The happiness that was building up within him poured forth as Gabe vowed, "Oh, I will; I sure will!"

XI

A Horse for the
Best Hunter

AFTER two days of comfortable travel through the canyon of the Madison and down its wide grassy valley, the Yellowstone Expedition of 1870 split up on Thursday, September 22. General Washburn and his party bade farewell to Lieutenant Doane and the five soldiers who were anxious to report back to Fort Ellis by nightfall. Elwyn Bean, his helper, and Nute would accompany the pack train north to Helena while the businessmen took a more roundabout route through Virginia City, Montana Territory.

"You come with us," Washburn told Gabe. "Now that we've got our park campaign lined up, you'll want to see us put it into action."

So Gabe, his ragged, soiled buckskins flapping on his lean frame, rode Tibo across tall grass and prickly pear to the top of the Gravelly Range, and then, after a last brief look at the distant peaks of the Yellowstone, descended into the mining camp. Jim Bridger had told him a good deal about the alder-lined gulch where prospectors had uncovered a gold bonanza and how within weeks ten thousand men were scratching and fighting for the gold that could be washed from the rich gravel in the creek bed.

Ugh! What an ugly place! The stampeders had stripped the hillsides of timber and brush and turned the gulch and lateral creeks upside down in their frantic scramble for gold. The road into town was rutted and crooked, with cabins crowding on each side; behind them were the tell-tale mounds of waste dumps and network of flumes trickling water to the rockers and sluice boxes.

In the snarled traffic of freightwagons and woodcarts on the main street of the gulch, the Washburn party had to slow their pace. Miners, pounding the boardwalk or leaning against the crude store fronts, hats tipped low to shade their eyes against the sun, stared at them. Washburn laughed and said loud enough for his friends to hear, "I bet we're being taken for down-on-our-luck prospectors."

When a group of ladies eyed them askance, Stickney tried to pull his tattered pants about his legs. "We should have come in by a back street. We're not fit for ladies to see."

Gabe agreed. They really were a wild-looking bunch in their shrunken, faded, torn clothing, hair and beards long unbarbered, faces nut-brown, lips sun-blistered, all of them thin from hard travel and lean eating. Gabe's shoulders began to twitch as they rode the narrow crowded street; already he wanted to shake off the people and buildings. He disliked the town smell, compounded of outhouses, garbage pits, stables, and cow barns. Oh, for a clean whiff of the Yellowstone!

Because the men looked so rough, the hostler refused to stall and grain their horses until Langford produced a gold piece from his money belt. Gabe noticed the men didn't bother to unholster their rifles, but he did; the Winchester was going everywhere with him. There was little use shouldering his packsack; he had no wash kit and no extra clothing save the cold-weather jacket. He was very self-conscious about his ragged garments. That was another thing he disliked about towns; you had to be thinking all the time about how you looked, because people judged you by your appearance more than by what you really were.

"I'm going directly to the telegraph office and wire Helena of our safe arrival here," Langford told them all. "And I'll also wire George Pritchett to get right on with that search for Everts."

"Be sure our families are notified," Hedges advised as he started down the street. When Gabe stood, rubbing one foot against the other, at a loss what to do, Hedges called, "Come on, young fellow."

Gabe trailed his friend into a littered, dusty, poorly lighted shop. Here the Judge chose wool pants and flannel shirts, stockings, and boots for himself and Gabe. Gabe was uneasy. He not only had never had "store" clothes before, but he had no money. He tugged on the Judge's sleeve. "I don't reckon I better get anything," he said, his face flushing with embarrassment.

"I'm buying your clothes," the Judge explained, and when he saw Gabe object he added, "This is my way of

159

saying thank you for all the extra work you had with that balky horse of mine. You're not beholden to me, lad; you've earned a new suit, and more."

Although Gabe was willing to accept the new clothes on these terms, he backed away from the new boots. When the Judge asked him to try them on for size, Gabe borrowed a rag from the storekeeper and washed his feet at the pump. Then he put them on and clumped up and down the aisle. The stiff leather barked his ankles; the strings cut off his circulation; they felt worse than hobbles. How was he not to seem ungrateful? "They're sure different from moccasins," he said politely, but with no enthusiasm.

The Judge laughed. "Somehow boots don't look right on you." He turned to the clerk. "Would you have some good moccasins in stock?" The clerk did, and Gabe's face wreathed in smiles as he slipped them on.

"Now for a bath," the Judge said as he paid for the purchases and carried them, unwrapped, in his arms.

A bath? Where? The creek was right in the middle of the town!

Swallowing his discomfort, Gabe followed the Judge, who soon turned into a barbershop. What a fancy place, with green plush chairs and shelves full of shaving mugs and barber bottles. The barber, swathed in a calico bib, handed each of them a towel and led the way to partitioned stalls, each containing a long, high, narrow tin tub and a chair. The barber turned on the spigot over the hot water tank, tested it, dropped a bar of yellow soap in the tub, and left.

Gabe scratched his nose while he studied the white man's bath; he didn't know they bathed in a horse trough!

After shucking his buckskins, he swung one leg over the rim, then the other, and lowered himself cautiously. He had never bathed in warm water, but it felt wonderful. He washed his hair and scrubbed himself with the stiff brush and stinging soap and sloshed, as much for fun as for rinsing. Then he stepped out and dabbed himself dry with the skimpy towel.

The cotton underdrawers were nothing new; he had worn them in wintertime. When he picked up the stiff wool trousers, bright red straps fell to the floor. Suspenders! Ayeeee, how he had hankered for these! He slipped the loops into the buttons on the trouser waistband, but something was wrong. They crisscrossed oddly, so he tried again and again and again, until the perspiration rolled down his forehead. He was irritated; he had learned to throw a diamond hitch; why couldn't he manage these things? Because he was quiet so long the Judge called, "I'm dressed. How are you doing?"

Gabe stuck his head outside the burlap curtain. "I be hornswoggled if I can figger out these suspenders."

Trying not to laugh, Hedges solved the puzzle. Gabe pulled on the trousers; after he put on the shirt and tucked the ends in, the Judge placed the unsnarled red straps over his shoulders. Gabe snapped them a few times and almost tied himself in knots seeing himself front and back. The moccasins were fine, but what was he supposed to do with the black socks? He thought hard, then grinned. Quickly he tied them into a headband, combed his hair with the comb hanging by a cord on the wall, and patted the soft cloth in place.

Resplendent in his new outfit, he buckled on the cartridge belt and knife sheath, picked up the rifle, and stepped out of the stall. While the barber trimmed the Judge's hair and beard, Gabe leaned against the wall, proudly snapping his suspenders. Next he followed his friend to the hotel and up to the room they would share. He was reluctant to leave the rifle and cartridge belt until Hedges showed him how they could lock the door so their belongings would be safe while they ate at the restaurant.

When they entered, the Judge headed for a large round table covered with a red checkered cloth. He was greeted by a young man who looked like a plucked turkey and who had a streak of white forehead showing where his hat had protected his skin from the sun. Gabe's hand flew to his mouth to cover his amazement. This was Walter Trumbull.

When Gabe sat down at his place, he knotted his hands in his lap. There were several pieces of hardware in front of him. He felt lost without his broad-bladed knife. No matter; if he wore white man's suspenders, he would have to get used to fork and spoon and eating at a table. He fidgeted; all of a sudden he didn't know what to do with his elbows.

But then Langford came in, smelling like that barbershop, and crowing over having lost thirty-five pounds.

"Me, too," the Judge added, "and I lost it all right here!" He pointed to his stomach. "I haven't been this flat since I walked from Independence, Missouri, to Virginia City seven years ago." The others that came in looked strange, too, and there was much laughter until General Washburn showed up. He looked like a bag of bones; the wattles on his chin shook when he coughed; his cheekbones were the wrong kind of red. But he was cheerful and talkative and ordered the biggest steak on the menu.

Gabe sawed away at his meat with the dull table knife, wishing he had thought to bring along his honing stone. He wolfed down the boiled potatoes and carrots, several pieces of bread spread half an inch thick with butter and jelly, plus everything the others didn't eat, and topped it off with four pieces of apple pie. The coffee was strong, but too thin; he missed the grounds floating in it. When the toothpicks were passed, he took one and watched how some of the men let theirs hang on their lips while they talked. It took a couple of tries before he got the right "hang" on his.

About the time the men lighted their cigars, a stranger came to the table and introduced himself as the reporter for the Virginia City newspaper, *The Madisonian*. The men made room for him so he could write in his notebook, and then they talked and talked and talked about the Yellowstone, until Gabe thought he had grown fast to the hard chair. Judge Hedges explained his idea about making the Yellowstone into a national park, and the reporter's pencil flew across the lined paper. So this was how you started working toward a national park!

It was very late when Gabe stumbled to the hotel and dropped down on the bed. The Judge was snoring in a few minutes, but Gabe could not sleep. The bed had a U sag in it, and the mattress was lumpier than a bedground of bunch grass. Finally he put a blanket on the floor, rolled in it, and fell asleep.

The next morning the men left early for Helena, riding out into a crisp, sunny day. Gabe was glad to leave the stink of the town behind him. Before long he was out where he could see and smell trees and grass again. Tibo was full of pepper and kicked up plenty of dust at first, but soon settled down to the long haul back over the Gravellies, down the Madison, north to the three forks where the Madison, Gallatin, and Jefferson came together to form the mighty Missouri. Since it was 120 miles northward to Helena, the party spent two nights at way stations and rode into Helena midday Tuesday, September 27. There the men split up, all hurrying to their homes except Langford, who was eager to get to his office. "Think you can find your way to Bean's stable?" he asked Gabe.

Gabe nodded. The Judge and Hauser had offered him lodging in their carriage houses, but he had already accepted Bean's offer to sleep at the stable and work there for his board and three dollars a month. That way he could tarry a while longer in Helena, be close to Tibo, and keep an ear to the ground on this national park business. The wrangler loaned him some old pants and a shirt so he could keep his new clothes clean. The days slipped by happily for him.

What an uproar there was over the expedition! The reports by Langford, Hauser, Washburn, and Hedges filled the front pages of the *Helena Herald* day after day. After their chores were done at night, Bean would read every word to Gabe. "Thet Langford's a fair wrangler with words," Bean would say every now and then as he read the emotional, elaborate descriptions of the headwaters country. Soon the newspapers from other towns in the Territory were reprinting the columns, and then those from as far away as Minneapolis, Chicago, St. Louis, and

New York. Gabe saved them all for Bridger, since he need carry little else in his saddlebag.

For a while Jake bragged around how he'd fought grizzlies and saved the expedition from all sorts of dangers, until his friends told him, "Go soak your head in Alum Creek." After that he didn't show any interest in the park idea.

Now the whole country knew Bridger was no liar, and what a wonderland the Yellowstone was; best of all, the park idea was really finding favor.

The greatest day of all was October 15, when George Pritchett telegraphed Mr. Langford, "EVERTS IS FOUND ALIVE BUT WASTED IN FLESH." After he had recovered and returned to Helena, the men gave a banquet in his honor. Gabe, scrubbed until he shone, with his suspender buckles glistening, sat open-mouthed as the kindly old man told of his "thirty-seven days of peril" in the Yellowstone; how he wandered alone, without a horse or gun, through forests and geyser basins, surviving the blizzard by huddling under a shelter of pine branches piled between two hot pools, subsisting on thistle roots as he groped half-blind all the way back north, almost to the Gardner River where he was found by Pritchett.

Then one frosty November morning Langford turned up unexpectedly at the stable and told Gabe that he was leaving within an hour for the east by stagecoach. "I'll be lecturing in Minneapolis, Chicago, Detroit, and New York City before going on to Washington to help petition for the national park. We've got to work fast. I heard just yesterday that in the spring two men expect to file claims on the geyser basin and cut the timber there. The sooner our petition becomes a law the better."

"I sure do wish you luck," Gabe told him. He thought a moment, and then hauled the precious yellow bead, his lucky piece, his magic talisman, from his knife sheath where it had lain so many weeks. "If it would help any, you can have this."

Langford was pleased, and he accepted the small bead pried from the rim of a hot spring. "I'll keep it right here in my vest pocket, and every time I get to thinking things aren't going our way, I'll rub it between my fingers. How's that?"

"Fine!" Gabe was thrilled. "Now I know everything will come out all right."

There was much that could happen to keep them from getting their park, Langford explained, particularly if the water power and timber interests lobbied against the petition. Gabe didn't know what "lobby" meant, but he did know one thing: since his dream about Mr. Everts had proved to be true, he was positive his vision would not fail either. "As long as you're leaving town, I reckon I better drift back to see Bridger. But I'm comin' back in the spring. Mr. Bean says likely we'll be wrangling another party up the Yellowstone."

"I don't doubt it." Mr. Langford offered his hand. "It's good-by for now, until spring. Give my regards to Bridger. Tell him I said he couldn't have sent a better man in his place. . . . By the way, how are you going back east? The steamboats aren't running this late."

"I'll walk," Gabe answered simply. How else could he go since he didn't own a horse?

Langford shook hands with him hard, then moved on for a brief word with Bean. Before departing, he called back, "Tell Bridger that without those lies of his we'd never have gone up the Yellowstone!" Then he waved and was gone.

Gabe blinked. He'd never thought of that. Without all those fantastic stories and except for him and Langford getting all excited over proving whether or not Bridger was lying, the Yellowstone might have existed unnoticed for years and years and then maybe have been discovered by a bunch of land-grabbers. . . . Say, they owed a lot to Bridger!

He wandered to where Bean was repairing a saddle. "All right with you if I leave tomorrow?"

"Yup," Bean answered as he sewed the tough leather.

"I sure do thank you for all you've done for me and for offering me a job for next year."

The wrangler smiled. "You earned your way. I'm much obliged to you for a lot of help."

Gabe looked out into the corral where Tibo was scratching himself on the snubbing post. "I'm sure going to miss Tibo. Can I ride him again next year?"

"Reckon so. He's your horse."

Not really my horse, Gabe knew; I trained him and rode him, and we get along very well, but it will be years before I can save up enough money to buy him. Wistfully he asked, "D'you suppose Tibo will know me in the spring?"

Bean pursed his lips. "Don't know why not, seein' as you two will be winterin' together."

"We'll be wh-at?"

"I tol' you, Gabe. Tibo is your horse." Trying not to grin, the wrangler drawled, "Leastaways, I think that's what Langford meant when he tol' me to give that pinto to the best danged hunter on the expedition."

When the good news struck home, Gabe leaped in the air. "You mean I got me a horse of my own?" Then he vaulted the gate and ran toward the little horse, shouting, "Ayeeee! Tibo! We're going to see ol' Bridger. Together!"

XII

Yellowstone National Park

ELEVEN months later, in the third week of July, 1871, Gabe returned to the Yellowstone River. "*Ah hi e*," he greeted the foaming green torrent as he shucked his buckskins and moccasins and waded into the icy water. It was so good to be back, looking upcanyon beyond the great Snowies, across Trail Creek where he had camped before, feeling the pull of the headwaters country in his heart.

He ducked up and down, the water running in his eyes and mouth, laughing, splashing, dog-paddling, until he was blue with cold; then in one leap he jumped to the bank. He ran a race in place to dry off and flapped his arms, wishing he could fly right to the falls. As he pulled on his buckskins, he was proud that the leggings were longer, the shirt broader through the shoulders. His store clothes and the precious suspenders were in his saddlebag.

He didn't know exactly what he was saving them for, but buckskins were better for mountain travel.

While he had spent the winter spinning many a yarn with Bridger, his Montana friends had worked hard for the park idea. In keeping Bridger informed, Langford had written, "Thanks to my lectures, an important chief scientist, a Federal Survey Director, is going to move his 'boys' up the Yellowstone come summer and prove that *I* am not a liar!"

Bridger almost doubled up laughing when he read that. "Now thar's a twist of the tobacco chew, calling Langford a liar." He read on: "Langford says there's no chance of Congress voting on a national park petition until after a federal survey of the headwaters. He says I know this scientist, Dr. Ferdinand Vandeveer Hayden. Why, shore I do! A two-legged grasshopper, that one. He knows his mountains. The Indians call him 'Picks Up Stones Running.'"

"Is he an Indian?" Gabe asked.

"Nope. But danged if he don't head up the weirdest tribe of bug catchers an' rock collectors. You'll see."

"I'll see? How?"

"Come summer. Langford has arranged for you to guide this here Hayden up the Yellowstone."

So here I am, Gabe thought happily as he finished dressing. He wished Langford and especially the Judge and Elwyn Bean were along, but aside from Lieutenant Doane who was in charge of the military escort again, Gabe was the only one of the 1870 party present. According to his way of thinking, Langford was making a real sacrifice: he was staying in steamy, hot Washington to work for the petition, instead of accompanying Hayden up the Yellowstone. The others wouldn't leave their jobs, and General Washburn was dead, "of the rigors of the Yellowstone," Langford had written, though Gabe thought it was the cough that killed him. Too bad; the Yellowstone had made an unusually nice person out of the General.

As soon as Gabe had climbed the steep riverbank he broke into a run, his moccasins hissing over the grass. He could see the breakfast fire smoking heavily. Potato John, the cook, wouldn't like it if Gabe wasn't on hand to carry the water and fire the *stove*. He was used to the stove by now; he'd been cutting wood for it all the way up from Ogden, Utah, where he had met Hayden and his tribe of scientists.

Bridger was right: what a tribe they were. It took him weeks to memorize their names: Naturalist, Ornithologist, Geologist, Meteorologist, Mineralogist, Zoologist, Botanist, and Herpetologist. There was another tribe represented also, the Surveyors, though they didn't look like blood brothers; and an Artist who was very good at picture writing, and a medicine man who worked magic with a black box and glass plates—a Photographer he was, though the men called him Bill Jackson.

But the chief, Hayden, was the most unusual of all. He was a little brown man with eyes like squaw's beads, always on the trot, always picking up rocks. Hayden talked the strangest gibberish, using words like lava, gneiss, basalt, granite, travertine, pudding stone, rhyolite. They made no sense to Gabe until Hayden explained they referred to different kinds of rock making up the floor of the valley and the mountains of the Yellowstone. Hmph! Why couldn't Hayden call a rock a rock, whether it was white, red, or brown, and let it go at that?

And the equipment these scientists carried! He'd been told, "Don't touch that. Keep away from here. Watch your step," until he walked as if he were in rattlesnake country. Sometimes, however, they let him peer through a microscope, or look at the theodolite, or hold the barometer or thermometer, but the most puzzling object of all was a two-wheeled thing for measuring distance. These scientists weren't satisfied to say Trail Creek was two sleeps away from the Gardner.

In addition they had more boxes for their bugs and mounted birds and animal skins, and lap desks, and blankets, and the usual guns, ammunition, tents—and food enough for an Army. They brought enough to sway the backs of twenty mules, not counting each man's saddle and pack horse, and the loading and unloading kept a half-dozen wranglers busy. Gabe helped the cook and cut firewood, but mostly he was the guide, together with Lieutenant Doane, and he was the *official* hunter of the Hayden Expedition. He would even be paid thirty dollars just for doing what he wanted all summer!

Panting slightly, Gabe stopped alongside the portable flat-topped iron stove, now belching smoke through its standpipe. Potato John, who never spoke unless it was absolutely necessary, pointed to the coffeepot and water cans. Gabe grabbed them and raced to the creek. Although he missed Nute and Booby, he thought Potato John was a good cook, and he owned a red retriever that had been trained to bring in wild fowl after they were shot down. Red was everybody's pet, but Gabe was the only one who ran races and rolled in the grass and wrestled with him.

"Morning!" A good many of the scientists greeted Gabe

as he passed them, careful to get water upstream from where they were washing or watering their horses. That was another thing that was different this summer: these men looked after their own stock and they really traveled fast; there was no dawdling along at five to ten miles a day. There was a lot of joking, and singing after supper, but during the day they were a serious bunch.

As Gabe made the first round with the coffeepot, Dr. Hayden asked, "What's ahead for us today?"

Gabe's chest swelled a little under his shirt. He knew Dr. Hayden had a report made up of the diaries of Langford and Washburn, as well as a copy of the military report which Lieutenant Doane had submitted to the War Department; yet he never failed to ask Gabe about the country they would cross each new day. So Gabe told him how the valley would grow narrow and the timbered spurs from the west cut more and more across their path; how to watch for the Crows, whose signals—fire by night and smoke by day—had already been seen on the mountaintops. "As long as you like rocks, you'll want to see Cinnabar Mountain; least, that's what Sam Hauser called it."

Hayden's eyebrows arched. "Cinnabar, eh? Good, good!"

They moved on up the valley often knee-deep in black-eyed daisies, wild flax, and red shooting star, breathing the flower and pine scented air. Gabe pointed to Emigrant Peak, and Hayden exclaimed enthusiastically to the other advance riders, "Marvelous example of a volcanic cone." Later Hayden grew enthusiastic about some plain old rocks, "Beautiful example of uplifted strata. Note that nearly vertical wall of quartzite on our right." Gabe

173

gave up trying to understand the scientist's tribal jargon, but he memorized the words, saying them over and over in his mind. Next year, when he was guiding another party up the Yellowstone, he'd want to say things like that so his party would think he was a pretty smart fellow!

Gabe found a safe fording across the swift Gardner River, and while waiting for the mule train to catch up he suggested, "Whyn't we explore up the Gardner aways? We didn't do it last year."

Hayden peered upcanyon. "Good idea." He slapped his heels on Patsy's flanks and led the way, Gabe, Bill Jackson, Moran, the artist, and several of the scientists trailing him. Before long he pointed to the canyon walls and shouted back over the noise of the water, "Volcanic rock. Looks like the refuse from an old furnace." Soon they left the river, rode up through a draw to the top of rounded hills, and here they reined up "in full view of one of the finest displays of nature's architectural skill the world can produce," Hayden wrote later in his scientific report. Ahead Gabe saw a white mountain resembling a cascade of frozen snow jeweled with the colored waters of many hot springs.

Hayden rode pell-mell to the foot of the glistening white hill whose steep sides were "ornamented with a series of semicircular basins, with margins varying in height and beautifully scalloped and adorned with a sort of beadwork . . . with every variety of shade of scarlet, green, and yellow. . . ."

Gabe thought the hill looked like a geyser basin lying on its side, with a hundred tinted pools lifting steamy ribbons to the sky. Where the water poured from the springs at the top, in a gentle dripping from one terrace to another, the beaded edges bore more colors than a field of wild flowers.

"You didn't see this last year?" Hayden asked Gabe.

"No, sir! And I bet Bridger never stumbled onto it or he would have told me."

Dismounting, the men explored on foot, Hayden running here and there as usual, exclaiming, "Good, good! Then I guess we can take credit for discovering the most fabulous hot springs terrace in America. Even if we don't see another thing the expedition will have been worth the trouble."

"Oh, you'll see lots more," Gabe assured him. "This here Yellowstone is plumb full of surprises."

The scientists scrambled like monkeys all over the terraces; they dipped thermometers in the pools and took specimens of the rock. Jackson, the photographer, set up his box on a tripod, ducked under a black cloth, reappearing shortly with a square plate covered by a wet towel, and immediately crawled into a small tent which he said was his portable darkroom to "develop the picture." Although Gabe had seen Jackson take innumerable pictures on the way up from Ogden, he was still awed by all this rigmarole.

When Jackson finally emerged he called Gabe and the others to see the first picture ever taken in the Yellowstone. "Ayeeee," Gabe murmured softly as he looked at the wet piece of paper. He could see the sparkling cascades and pools and almost feel the grainy beading of the rimrock. The only things lacking were the delicate colorings of the terrace walls and the smells—the hot mineral breath of the springs and steam, the burnt ground, and the encircling scrub cedar, sage, and juniper.

"What are you going to do with that picture?" he asked Jackson, who was a young man, agile as a deer, friendly, and talkative.

The photographer smiled. "If you were trying to describe these mammoth hot springs to some one who had never seen them, which do you think would be better, words or this photograph?"

"That!" Gabe almost shouted, pointing a brown finger at the picture. "Golly, with that you don't need words. It says most everything."

Jackson seemed pleased. "Exactly! And after I have put together a whole folio of pictures of the Yellowstone and presented them for the Congressmen to see, don't you think they'll fall over themselves passing that bill to preserve all these natural wonders?"

Gabe hoped so. But he was worried. Bridger had told him that if Congress set aside the headwaters country as a national park, a paper would be drafted saying so, and Mr. President Grant would sign it, and it would be the law.

"That paper," Gabe had asked the pathfinder. "Would it be kind of like a treaty?" He knew all about treaties; the Shoshone chiefs were forever "touching the stick," signing them. A treaty was an agreement between enemies that there would be no more fighting; the white men gave the Indians blankets and kettles and cornmeal, and the Indians gave the white men their hunting grounds for settlement.

Bridger had answered, "Yep, that's what it be! A treaty,

176

between the govmint and the people to protect the Yellowstone."

Gabe's face had sobered. He knew what the white men did with treaties; they ignored them and went right on settling on the land and killing the buffalo and warring on the Indians. When he mentioned this, Bridger tried to quiet his fears by saying, "Likely they'll name someone to look after this park and enforce the treaty. An' they'll appoint a guard or two to catch the timber thieves and game poachers."

For one wild, sweet moment Gabe wished he could be a guard; then his vision would all come true, and he'd be spending the rest of his life in the Yellowstone.

Unknowingly Bridger dashed his hopes. "Likely they'll bring in a passel of soldiers to guard the place."

But Gabe could not feel stone-hearted as he gazed first at Jackson's fine pictures and later at the bold colored sketches painted by the artist, Thomas Moran, a tall, lean, quiet man who went fishing whenever he wasn't painting. Gabe was sure that after people saw the photographs and paintings they would surely throng to the Yellowstone. His heart lifted as he realized that the travelers would need wranglers and packers and a guide. He'd settle for being one, or all three, and he'd promise Mr. President Grant to hunt only enough elk and deer to keep his party in meat. He wouldn't remove nearly as many animals as would die anyway in the natural life of the forest.

Thus, as he stood with the enthusiastic Hayden and his tribesman at the brink of Tower Falls, the Grand Canyon and falls, and the lake, Gabe was content.

Speaking about a show-off, that Yellowstone beat all. Because he was seeing the high country a month earlier than he had last time, Gabe found meadows purple with slender harebells, wild iris, lupine, and columbine; higher up, close to the snowbanks, there were slopes carpeted in yellow glacier lily and globe mallow. The creeks sang full-throated; the weather was excellent; there were few flies and mosquitoes; and the men worked hard and in high spirits from dawn to dusk in this "collector's paradise," as they called it.

Only Gabe was able to keep up with Hayden as the latter led them a merry chase up and down mountains and ferreted out hidden lakes and waterfalls and remote clearings where deer and antelope looked at them and after sniffing and flapping their ears lowered their heads to graze, undisturbed by their alien presence. "You're right," Hayden told Gabe. "Our wild friends deserve a refuge. We must not fail them. I'll see that a 'no hunting' provision—one to forestall commercial hunting—is tacked onto that petition."

At night, when the men gathered around the fire to sing and talk, Gabe was often called upon to relate Bridger's "windies" about the jewel tree, the pool with the fire burning in the bottom, the hot and cold river, and the glass mountain, which Gabe had located south of the Mammoth Hot Springs. It proved to be a mountain of obsidian, the black-brown volcanic glass prized by the Indians for arrowheads. At first Gabe was shy in his story telling, but after he got used to the men he tried to tell the stories as Bridger told them, in the crude, humorous mountain-man jargon, and his audience roared its approval.

Gabe was always aware of Hayden watching him with a friendly eye, questioning him for his knowledge of the

Yellowstone, complimenting him on his controlled hunting and his Indian and white man's know-how in camping comfortably in the wilderness. As Gabe gained confidence in the man, he told him about his vision and was overjoyed to see the scientist take it seriously. Once Hayden said, "Civilization must not take its toll of the Yellowstone"; and another time, "We're going to have to find a way to keep you and the Yellowstone together."

Ho! Gabe thought; wouldn't that be marvelous?

When the riders and pack train labored through the forest to the Firehole, Gabe pointed out the trail to the north and then galloped ahead alone. He couldn't wait to see his friend, Old Faithful. Sure enough; he had just picketed Tibo under the trees and run out to greet the geyser, when it rumbled a welcome and then celebrated his return with a dazzling eruption. *"Ah hi e!"* Gabe shouted as the water soared higher and higher.

When the geyser quieted, Gabe looked anxiously around the basin, then sighed with relief. So far, there had been no loggers slashing the forests along the Firehole.

When Hayden and his men arrived, they poured off their horses and scrambled around the basin like men pursued by bees. The geysers really put on a show: something was always popping, dancing, erupting, growling, steaming, splashing—a water symphony, Hayden called it. The colors blazed brighter than ever under the blue sky; the sunset colors vied with those of the pools; the scientists were in a frenzy of note-taking, and took plenty of time exploring a middle and lower geyser basin and all sorts of "sideshows." They just couldn't get over the pool with the "fire" burning in the bottom.

The weeks slipped by quickly and although no blizzard tented the party, the aspen and wild rose leaves began turning yellow and red-bronze, the nights were cold, and there was ice on the water buckets. The nearer the time came to leave the Yellowstone, the more the scientists complained; they hadn't seen half enough, their notebooks and collections weren't nearly completed, they must have at least one more summer in the Yellowstone.

One morning Hayden said to Gabe, "I've made up my mind to return here next summer. Since it is very expensive to transport our equipment back to Ogden, I've been wondering: if we cached it up near the Mammoth Hot Springs, would you be willing to guard it for us? It would mean spending the winter alone, but we'd see you had a good shelter and plenty of food."

"I'd sure like that!" Gabe replied quickly. "And I wouldn't mind being alone. I'd have Tibo to keep me company."

Hayden grinned. "Potato John has offered to leave Red with you."

Gabe had a hard time to stifle his yelp of joy. A horse, and a dog, and the Yellowstone. What more could a mountain man want?

So the scientists returned to the Mammoth Hot Springs, and in a place sheltered from the north wind by a timbered hill, but open enough to be warmed by the winter sunshine, they built weather-tight sheds for their tents and spare equipment and a snug little cabin with a good fireplace. They even fashioned Gabe a table and chair and a bunk for his thick layer of quilts and left an axe and saw, cooking utensils, and more than enough staple groceries which he would supplement with game meat and fowl.

Gabe was sorry to see the men leave, their mules laden with specimens and notebooks, the most sure-footed animal carrying Jackson's precious glass plates. But he was thrilled to have the Yellowstone all to himself.

The long wait began. . . .

With a joyful heart, Tibo and Red running freely alongside him, he cut and stacked an enormous pile of firewood. Then he cut wild grass and shaved cottonwood bark for Tibo. The golden cottonwood leaves flamed briefly, then wind and snow stripped the branches. He watched the elk, deer, and antelope sprout winter coats and wide wings of geese fly southward, though a good number stayed near the warm springs all winter.

He had sniffed out the blizzard a day before it howled over the basin and was ready for it. But there were warm middays and time to build a lean-to onto his cabin for Tibo and fashion snowshoes for himself. Many nights were filled with the small hissing of snowfall, and many days were all white below and blue above, with time to make himself a new buckskin suit and moccasins, to melt snow water, and improve on his biscuit making. . . .

One morning he woke to the music of icicles thawing. Gradually the snow retreated to the forest cover, and the Gardner began to run again; bears, gaunt from hibernation, emerged half-blind and scratched their backs on the trees; carpet pink and purple pasqueflower glowed on the sunny hillsides.

But not until the grass was hock high on Tibo did Gabe hear the clop-clop-clop of an approaching pack train; there were Chief Hayden and his tribesmen again!

Ho! What a reunion they all had!

"How you've grown!" Hayden greeted him.

"What a big man you growed up to be all of a sudden," Potato John said in a rare spate of words.

Gabe roasted a fine buck for them and welcomed them back to the Yellowstone. Later on, when all gathered around the open campfire and it was like old times, Hayden told Gabe, "Well, we pulled it off, and it was Jackson's photographs that did the trick. The boys and I talked up the Yellowstone; we shoved reports under the Congressmen's noses; but we didn't get anywhere, nor did your friend, Langford. He and the Montana Territorial delegate, a Mr. Clagett, worked hard, but they didn't have any luck either. Congress wasn't interested in a national park; they didn't want any part of the mountain country closed to settlement and lumbering.

"Then Langford and I personally called on every senator and representative and every bigwig we thought might help us, but it was no use. Then the day, the very morning, the Congressmen were to vote on the national park bill, Bill Jackson placed a folio of his Yellowstone views on every legislator's desk. . . . Gabe," Hayden exclaimed, "I only wish you could have been with me in the gallery, to watch those men walk in, joshing and talking back and forth, taking their places at their desks, and opening those folios! They stopped talking; they sat down and turned over those magnificent pictures one by one. They scarcely raised their heads to answer roll call. When the enabling act—the petition for the national park—was read, they all voted AYE! and then applauded themselves! Then the bill was rushed to President Grant, and on March second* he signed it. Now our country has her first national park!"

* 1872

Gabe exhaled noisily; he hadn't dared breathe all the time Hayden was talking for fear the story might not end as he had prayed it would. "Ayeeee," he murmured over and over, joy mushrooming within him, until he thought he would burst. And to think it all started with Jim Bridger's storytelling!

"And that's not all," Hayden continued. "Your friend Langford was appointed the first superintendent of our first national park. When he took the oath of office he vowed to protect the Yellowstone from timber thieves and souvenir collectors, but one thing he didn't swear to, because he said that would be your job."

"My job?" Gabe exclaimed, his voice squeaky with excitement.

"When Langford found out he could have one assistant, he appointed you as the first guard of the new park. He said you'd know what to do."

Gabe leaped to his feet, his heart thumping, his mind filled with his vision and the long, happy future.

"*I* know what to do. It'll be my job to hold back the hunter!"

Author's Note

IN the history of the Yellowstone River headwaters country, the snow months of 1807-1808 are important. It was then that John Colter set out on one of the most remarkable solitary explorations in history. A former member of the Lewis and Clark Expedition, Colter was dispatched by Manuel Lisa from his new fur trading post at the mouth of the Big Horn River on the lower Yellowstone to invite the Crow nation, and others, to trade at his wilderness outpost.

At first on horseback and later on foot and snowshoes, Colter traveled southward up the Big Horn and Shoshone, crossed the Continental Divide, skirted Jackson Lake and the Tetons, and then turned northward across the Divide once more, entering what is now Yellowstone National Park. According to a map sketched months later by William Clark from Colter's account of his journey, he swung around present-day West Thumb Bay of Yellowstone Lake, followed the west bank of the river downstream across Hayden Valley and the adjacent thermal basins, did not see the Grand Canyon and Falls of the Yellowstone because of heavy timber, and after locating

185

the Great Trail of the Indians above Tower Creek, topped the mountainous barrier on the northeast and dropped back down the Big Horn to Fort Manuel. Because he described smoking pits and an all-pervading "smell of brimstone" and more particularly a large boiling spring beyond the Park boundaries on the Stinkingwater, or Shoshone River, his trapper friends dubbed the region Colter's Hell. Although the name actually referred to the hot spring near present-day Cody, Wyoming, the term Colter's Hell soon included in the popular fancy the entire headwaters of the Yellowstone.

Undoubtedly other trappers and mountain men must have visited the area at a later date, but not until September 27, 1827, do we have published in the *Philadelphia Gazette* and reprinted October 6 in the *Niles Weekly Register* (Baltimore) an eyewitness account written by trapper Daniel T. Potts of his visit in July to the lake and to several of the thermal basins.

James Bridger, a noted trapper and guide, first visited the Park region in 1830. He soon added his own stories to both the facts and fantasies about the place, stories inspired by the natural wonders seen this year and on subsequent visits through the 1860's.

Nathaniel Pitt Langford tried unsuccessfully in 1868 and 1869 to organize an expedition to "authenticate or repudiate" the wonders of the Yellowstone. Although the Crow threat made his plans seem foolhardy, and official duties kept him from carrying through any action, three of the men who signed on for his 1869 expedition quietly left Helena in the late summer, visited Tower Falls, the Grand Canyon and Falls, the West Thumb, missed the Upper Geyser Basin, but did see the Lower Geyser Basin before following the Firehole to its junction with the Madison and continuing down the Madison to the Missouri, and finally back to Helena. Charles W. Cook, David E. Folsom, and William Peterson, so prided themselves on their reputations as men of veracity that they refused to speak publicly or write of their astonishing discoveries, although they are said to have spoken guardedly to Washburn and Langford and to have furnished the two leaders with a map of their route. The Yellowstone Expedition of 1870 fulfilled Langford's fondest hopes.

Following the federal survey under Dr. F. V. Hayden in 1871, President Ulysses S. Grant signed the Act of Dedication establishing Yellowstone National Park on March 1, 1872. Nathaniel Langford was rewarded for his labors by being appointed the first superintendent of the park, an office he filled diligently without pay until 1877.

Following the Hayden surveys, numerous other military and scientific explorations brought to light the thousands of thermal wonders and other natural beauties of Yellowstone National Park. In 1878 the second superintendent, P. W. Norris, built a road from Mammoth Hot Springs into Norris and Lower Geyser basins. By 1879 the Park had 90 miles of "travelable" roads; in the summer months wagons, carriages and sightseers were considerably in evidence, this in spite of occasional skirmishes with Bannock and Nez Percé Indians.

By 1883 the Northern Pacific Railway branch line was completed to within three miles of present-day Gardiner, Montana; Mammoth Hotel was under construction, and tent hotels were operating at the Lower and Upper Geyser basins and the Grand Canyon. Along with a rising tide of tourists were timber thieves and game poachers, but they wrought little damage. Between the United States Army Corps of Engineers and their crews building the roads and patrolling and a rash of hotel and "cottage" building, the lawbreakers found the Yellowstone too crowded to get away with large-scale operations. In addition to comprising one of the world's greatest thermal regions, with numerous outstanding geysers, the 3,471.51 square miles within the Park boundaries form one of the largest and most primitive wildlife refuges on the North American continent.

Between 1872 and 1895, not less than one thousand, nor more than five thousand, people visited the park annually. In 1895, when the first of annual travel tables began, the number had risen to 5,438. In 1957 1,595,875 persons visited the granddaddy of the national parks, topping a ten-year record of over one million visitors annually to Yellowstone. A multimillion dollar project is now under way to enlarge and improve tourist accommodations and camps and to extend the oiled highway Grand Loop Tour that traces the route of the 1870 Expedition.

Hold Back the Hunter is fiction, but is based on the events which occurred during the first organized exploration of the present park region. The Yellowstone Expedition of 1870, also widely known as the Washburn-Langford-Doane Expedition, resulted in a *first* in American conservation: the setting aside of the Upper Yellowstone country as our first national park and ultimately the establishment of our National Park Service. Much of the material for this book has been derived from diaries of the explorers and the Hayden surveys, early newspaper reports, and a detailed firsthand tracing of the expedition's route. Since the route of the 1870 Expedition was the foundation for the present Grand Loop Tour, this book serves as a story of adventure, a history, and a guidebook.

Although few liberties have been taken with the facts, it must be mentioned that of course the accomplishments of the 1870 Expedition are seen through the eyes of a fictional character, young Gabe Kirkpatrick. All other characters mentioned in the book are real, except that there were two Negro cooks instead of one. Nineteen men in all comprised the expedition, plus thirty-five horses and mules. Although there are now several entrances to the park, this book begins at the big bend of the Yellowstone River, now Livingston, Montana, long considered the "official" entrance to Yellowstone National Park.